GOTHAM™
CITY OF MONSTERS

JASON STARR

TITAN BOOKS

GOTHAM: CITY OF MONSTERS
Print edition ISBN: 9781785651472
E-book edition ISBN: 9781785651489

Published by Titan Books
A division of Titan Publishing Group Ltd
144 Southwark Street, London SE1 0UP

First edition: May 2018
10 9 8 7 6 5 4 3 2 1

TIBO40873

A CIP catalogue record for this title is available from the British Library.
Printed and bound in the United States.

GOTHAM
CITY OF MONSTERS

FOR MOM

GOTHAM
CITY OF MONSTERS

PROLOGUE

Fish Mooney thought this was it—the end. It wouldn't be the first time she'd died, but it would probably be the last. How ironic that she had survived assassination attempts and arcane experiments, only to die in a nuclear explosion. Spectacular, to be sure, but such a waste.

Just a few minutes earlier the future had seemed so bright. Thanks to whatever Hugo Strange had done to her, she had an amazing new ability—she could control a person's thoughts and actions just by touching them. A neon-green light, almost like a miniature aurora borealis, appeared at the point of contact and then—*voila!*—

Fish was in charge; the way it *should* be.

She'd already converted Hugo Strange's formerly bitchy-ass assistant, Ethel Peabody, into an obedient pussycat. It was nice to get some payback on Peabody, but more importantly she'd released Fish from her cell in the bowels of Arkham Asylum. Then Fish had freed as many of the other monsters as she could, just to create a good distraction, and made it to the garage.

Down here she smelled the smoggy-yet-exhilarating Gotham air—*ah, the sweet scent of freedom!* Then, just as she was about to leave, the metal garage door had slammed shut in front of her.

Just like that, Maria Mercedes Mooney was doomed again. Coincidence? Highly unlikely. No, Strange had activated lockdown procedures. He'd boasted of having a nuclear bomb, set to destroy all of the evidence and products of his experiments. One thing Fish had learned about the good doctor while under his "care"—the man was unpredictable, and capable of *anything*. If you thought you had him all figured out— *think again*.

For example, when Fish first heard about Strange's monsters and genetic experiments, she'd thought, *Yeah, right. Like* that *could ever happen*. She'd thought it was the ranting of a delusional megalomaniac, but, *oh yeah*, it had happened all right. Much, much worse, it had happened to *her*.

He'd claimed to fear what would happen if his monsters escaped. Did he really believe that monsters in Gotham would be worse than killing tens of thousands of innocent people in a nuclear blast? For that matter, did he give a rat's ass about the safety of the city? Not a chance. He only cared about himself and his so-called legacy. Nobody understood the mind of a crazed psychopath better than Fish.

After all, like they say, it takes one to know one, right?

Fish had many reasons to hate Strange. He'd brought her back from the sweet calm of death, just to turn her into a glorified lab animal. Like a dead frog, prodded with electricity! Certainly, he'd turned her into something more than human, but calling her a monster was too much. Maybe Strange's other subjects, or patients—call them what you will—were inhuman, but Fish Mooney wasn't a goddamn monster. She didn't have claws or animal-like teeth, or wings, or extra limbs like some of the freaks Fish had seen in the underbelly of Arkham.

Strange may have been insane, but he had a sense of humor.

No, Fish Mooney was Fish Mooney, and she'd always be Fish Mooney, bitch. No matter what Strange did to try to mess with her body and her mind.

As much as Fish hated Strange, she had to respect him for one thing—he'd brought her back to life. Maybe he hadn't done it out of the goodness of his heart, but a fact was a fact. Here she was. After the Penguin had thrown her off a roof into the Gotham River that should have been it. *Finite, sayonara.* Yet, lo and behold, Strange's people had "fished" her out of the river and Strange had done the impossible. He had *reanimated* her. In Gotham, it seemed, death wasn't the end.

Perhaps *an* end, but not necessarily *the* end.

Snapping out of her ill-timed reverie, Fish heard sirens in the distance—the GCPD heading to the scene. No matter. They'd arrive too late to save Gotham.

You've come this far, baby. Come on, think.

She looked around for something she could use to pry the gate open, but unfortunately there was nothing in the garage except an old bus. There wasn't enough time to go back into the main part of the asylum and search for another way out.

Then she noticed that the driver-side door to the bus was open. Stepping up and inside, she saw the key in the ignition. This was supposed to be *someone's* getaway ride, maybe even Strange's.

"Help us… Help us."

Who the hell was that, and where was it coming from? The voice—it sounded more like a growl—came from further back into the bus. Shadows shifted in the gloom, just out of sight.

Moving back outside, Fish went around to the back of the bus, and found the emergency exit open. It was dark, and difficult to see inside. As she got closer, she could hear heavy breathing and more voices, some growling like the first. Others resonated oddly, like birds or maybe reptiles.

"Help us… Help us… Help us."

As her eyes adjusted to the darkness, she could see further in. Several pairs of wild eyes stared back. Sure enough, there were monsters in there. Fish had seen some of them in the asylum, in cells and laboratories, but she hadn't realized there were so many. It was impossible to count them, and she didn't want to get close enough to try.

Returning to the gate she tried again to pry it open, to no avail.

Then, as the sirens were a block or two away at most, a red light flashed and the loudspeaker in the ceiling crackled to life.

"Security system deactivate."

The gate opened, all by itself.

Fish didn't know what had prompted this, or why, but she wasn't going to look a gift horse in the mouth. Moving quickly back to the bus, she turned the key, stubbornly ignoring the passengers she knew loomed behind her. The engine rumbled to life, their entreaties fell away, and she shifted into drive. Backing up, she turned the lumbering vehicle, then she floored it, peeling out of the garage.

Out to the rain-slicked streets of Gotham. This was *her* town. Not so long ago, she'd had a finger in the till of gambling, drinking, drugs, sex, and just about every other vice imaginable. Working with Carmine Falcone, she was well on her way to becoming one of the most canny and influential crime lords in Gotham. Then her protégé, Penguin, killed her.

For the moment she had no destination—she just wanted to get away. Maybe she'd get out of Gotham, to the countryside, then ditch the monster-filled bus. She didn't need that sort of baggage. So she drove down a ramp and spotted a chain-link fence, glittering in the rain-swept darkness.

What the hell? Nothing to lose...

Hitting the accelerator, she caused the bus to lurch toward the barrier and smash right through it. The fence gave way with a metallic screeching that set her teeth on end, then the pieces fell away and she was out on the streets. The sirens grew louder, and two Gotham City Police Department squad cars appeared on her tail, in hot pursuit. She clenched her jaw and gripped the wheel tighter. There was no way after coming this far, beating death, that Fish was going to let herself be caught.

Speeding onto the Petersburg Highway, she drove alongside the support pillars for the elevated subway tracks, picking up speed—but it wasn't enough. Glancing in the rearview, Fish saw the squad cars, still following, getting a little closer, their sirens blaring.

She smiled, loving every second of it. After all, getting chased by the cops felt so much better than being dead, or cooped up in that damn cell, getting treated like a lab rat by Hugo Strange and his crew of mad scientists. There wasn't heaven or hell when you died, just a whole lot of nothing, and that wasn't the way Fish Mooney rolled. She needed excitement. She needed action.

A car ahead of her slowed down, but she didn't follow suit. The bus had the advantage of size and bulk. Accelerating, she sideswiped the car. Sparks sprayed as it crashed into a roadside railing and spun out of control. Speeding past, Fish saw the aftermath in the rearview mirror. The car careened to a stop, blocking the road and forcing the police cars to screech to a halt. She grinned, still pointedly ignoring the shadows hunched in the seats behind her.

It was late enough that traffic was light. She exited onto South Burnside, still under the looming bulk of the elevated train, when a car turned the corner ahead of her, and she had to blink at the glare of blinding halogen headlights. Another car approached her, head-on. The driver had guts—she had to give them that. It was a real game of chicken.

Well, a bus versus a car. Fish liked her odds.

"Come to momma," she said.

With a gleefully crazed expression, she sped toward a head-on collision. Something pinged off the metal framework of the bus—what the hell, were those *bullets*? A spider web appeared in the windshield, then another. She was going to die—again. The car veered, skidded, then came the inevitable collision. The bus-car combination skidded along the road for a few seconds, then ground to a halt.

After a few dazed moments, Fish took stock. She wasn't dead. In fact, she wasn't even wounded. Maybe the experiments had left her stronger than ever. Maybe she was just damned *lucky*. Pulling herself out of the seat, she realized there was someone outside of the bus.

"Professor Strange." The voice was whiny, and one she recognized all too well. "Professor Strange!" It was Oswald Cobblepot—the Penguin. The man who pushed a wounded Fish Mooney into the river and killed her.

"Come out," Cobblepot said. "Strange, we need to talk."

If Penguin wanted "strange," he was going to get

"strange" all right. Fish climbed out of the smashed-up bus and stalked around the wreck, approaching Penguin from behind.

"You did a very bad thing to me," Penguin continued, "and now you're going to *pay*."

She tapped Penguin on the back. He wheeled around and, oh, that look of shock and horror was beyond priceless. His eyes went round and his mouth hung open, but nothing came out. This was what she'd craved ever since the moment Fish had been brought back to life. Maybe there were people in Gotham who feared Penguin, were intimidated by his power and ruthlessness, but Fish—better than anyone—knew what a coward the man truly was. He thought her death had made him the king of Gotham, but…

Surprise!

"Impossible," Penguin gasped.

Relishing the moment, Fish smiled. Then she touched Penguin's cheek. A flash of light appeared, thanks to the newfound ability still alive and strong within her.

"Nothing is impossible," she said.

Penguin fainted.

There was a sound. Fish turned and saw Butch Gilzean, another former employee, with several of his gangster pals. Butch was clutching a bazooka and looked almost as shell-shocked as the Penguin had been. Here was another coward disguised as a man. Gotham was full of them these days.

"Holy…" Butch gasped. "No."

He lowered the weapon, wisely respecting Fish's inherent authority. Butch was as dumb as a bag of nails, but he had to know that with Fish back, alive and well, the proper pecking order would return to Gotham. Instinctively, Butch knew his place.

He backed away several feet, and his friends followed his example. Then he turned and fled. They followed him, the clacking of their heels fading into the night. As she watched them run like little boys, Fish heard moaning inside the bus.

"Help... help."

You want help, Fish thought, *you're asking the* wrong *person.*

She began to move away from the bus, figuring the cops would deal with the mess. She had more important things to do. She'd been strong in her first life, stronger than almost any man in Gotham. Now, with her new ability, who would be able to stop her? Her new reality swept through her in a rush of power.

"Let the fun begin, baby," she muttered.

O N E

Five months later…

Selina Kyle arrived at Gotham Federal Bank on Powell Street at two twenty-four p.m. She had no idea why she'd been told to arrive at that particular time, or anything about the rest of the crew. She wasn't some idiot though—she knew the key to staying alive in Gotham: Don't ask too many questions, especially to the wrong people.

In Gotham, what you knew *could* hurt you. People who knew too much always seemed to wind up dead or missing.

She'd hooked up with this crew through the grapevine. "The grapevine" consisted of "people who aren't your friends and whom you never want to ever be your friends." Even so, they served a purpose, and Selina was just in it for the money anyway. She'd get a thousand bucks—five hundred before and five hundred after—not get-rich-quick money, but not bad for a few minutes' work. All she had to do was create a distraction at the appointed place and the appointed time.

The assignment had come from the one member of the crew she'd met—the guy who'd hired her. A scruffy, angry-looking, creepy killer-type guy, who'd probably been in and out of jail a dozen times or more, and maybe even spent time at Arkham. It was hard to have a career in crime without doing at least a couple stints at Blackgate or Arkham—in fact, it was like a badge of honor.

They'd met two days ago beneath an underpass in the northern outskirts of Gotham. Selina got there by hitching a ride on a motorcycle, while he came in a car. He told her what she had to do, how much she'd get paid. Trying to sound dangerous, Selina warned him that he'd better pay her, that if he even *thought* about double-crossing her, he was making a big mistake.

"I used to work for Fish Mooney, and Fish is back in town, back from the *dead*," she said ominously. "She's going to be the Queen of Gotham, you know. Me and Fish used to be like this… " She crossed her fingers. "So if you're thinking about messing with me, you better be thinking about messing with Fish Mooney too—which, trust me, isn't something you want to be doing. If you get my drift."

She wondered if she'd taken it too far, but the guy's expression said she'd made her point. Although she was just a teenager, Selina knew she was way brighter than most adults. Way savvier. Another trick to getting ahead in Gotham was associating with the right people. It didn't matter if you were Bruce Wayne or Selina Kyle, there was a pecking order leading to the top. If you wanted to get places you had to learn how to play the game.

You couldn't just sit on the sidelines.

He paid her the first five hundred.

Now, loitering in the bank lobby, Selina wore a black leather jacket, a black turtleneck, and a black wool hat. Black was Selina's favorite color, and she liked the way it camouflaged her at night. She could grab a guy's wallet, duck into an alley, and, *poof*, disappear. She'd heard somewhere that famous, powerful people, like presidents and business moguls, wore the same outfit practically all the time.

Selina doubted she'd ever be president. At sixteen years old she already had *way* too many skeletons for that. But powerful? Yeah, that was part of the plan, she thought as she approached the guard. Her eyes went wide, and she tried to look scared. She was a pretty good actress when she needed to be, which was pretty much all of the time.

"Help, my friend was just hit by a car," Selina said to the guard, sounding convincingly frantic. She was good at this.

"Where?" Selina pointed outside, to the right of the bank entrance. "You stay here," he said as he moved toward the revolving door. "I'll take care of it."

She watched through the plate-glass window as the

guard rushed outside and two guys wearing black ski masks grabbed him. One of the guys injected him with a sedative or something, and then they stuffed him into a van, sliding the door shut before anyone even noticed. Then the guys entered the lobby with guns drawn. It all happened in, like, five seconds—these guys knew what they were doing.

Her job was done, so it was time to hide in plain sight. Now, like everyone else in the bank—and there were maybe, like, thirty Gothamites in here—she was just along for the ride.

"This is a stickup," one of the masked guys announced. "Everybody face first on the floor." Selina recognized his voice—it was the creepy-looking man who'd hired her a few days ago. Putting on her scared face again, Selina got on the floor with the other people. The easiest way for her to get through this was to play the clueless victim—so opposite of who she really was, so she really had to use her acting skills.

So far there wasn't anything special about the gig. She figured the guys would rob the safe, take the money from the cashiers, and then they'd get away in the van. They'd dump the guard somewhere, and then Selina would meet up with them later to get the rest of her pay.

Then things stopped being normal.

She forced herself to suppress a shudder when, looking up, she saw two monsters enter the bank. At first, Selina had been as freaked out as the rest of the city by the monsters that had invaded Gotham, some five months back. It took a lot to freak Selina out, but she'd actually seen a couple of them, and photos of others in the newspapers. Some were so gross and disgusting, they were hard to look at.

After a while Selina had gotten used to the monsters and, as long they weren't bothering her, what difference did it make? Actually, the monsters had *helped* her. Thanks to all the chaos, and the police state Gotham had turned into, there weren't as many cops around to pay attention to smaller crimes, and Selina had been cleaning up.

Getting used to the monsters didn't make them any less frightening in person. All of them were different—at least they all had different features. These two were men, or used to be men when they were human. One of them was, like, seven feet tall, so maybe he used to be a basketball player or something. His skin was mostly tennis-ball green, with a texture like some kind of tree, and he had a ridge-like spine sticking out from his back.

The other monster was shorter and looked like a dog. Not because he was ugly—though he *was* ugly—but because he actually *looked* like a dog, with a snout and fangs. Even more than the tall one, he gave her the creeps. It was probably just an instinctual thing. Selina had always been more of a cat person.

A bunch of people shrieked when they saw the monsters.

Selina just rolled her eyes, muttering, "Holy jeez."

The leader of the crew fired his gun at the ceiling a couple of times.

"The next guy who screams, gets one between the eyes!" he announced. That should've shut everybody up, but there always seemed to be at least one dense person in the crowd. In this case it was a thin, old guy with a gray beard—he sort of looked like an anorexic Santa Claus. Anyway, he couldn't help whimpering.

The leader guy shot him between the eyes.

"Anybody else wanna meet their maker today?"

The bank went as silent as a library.

"I didn't think so."

Even Selina gaped at his brutality. *Great, it was supposed to just be a bank robbery*, she thought, *and now I'm an accessory to murder. Could this gig get any more messed up?*

The other guy—not the leader—went to a woman with long brown hair who was lying on the floor near the information desk.

"*You*, get up."

He sounded older than the leader. His voice was gravelly too, like a smoker. He was carrying a duffel bag.

The woman scrambled to her feet, eager to follow orders. She had a pin on her shirt—it said "Clarissa Morgan Bank Manager." She was pretty. The guy handed Clarissa Morgan Bank Manager the bag.

"Empty all the drawers as fast as you can, and then the safe," he growled. Then he pointed his gun directly at her. "If you try to push an alarm, *everybody* gets shot."

"Yes, sir, right away," the woman said.

Selina frowned.

There was a tone in her voice. It sounded like she

wasn't just talking, but that she was reading a line from a script. Probably everybody else in the bank had missed it, but not Selina. She picked up on stuff like that. Suddenly it made sense. Yeah, no doubt about it—the bank manager was part of the crew.

Clarissa Morgan went behind the plexiglass into the tellers' area. Selina couldn't see what the woman was doing, but figured she was filling the duffel bag with money.

She better not be getting more than me for this job. Her thoughts were interrupted by a loud voice from off to her right. It echoed through the lobby.

"Police, drop your weapons!"

Seriously?

Selina looked over at a nervous-looking guy in his twenties. He was in jeans and a hooded sweatshirt, but he was aiming a gun with one hand and flashing a GCPD badge with the other. He was an off-duty cop, or maybe undercover. With his wide-eyed, deer-in-headlights gaze, he looked like he was fresh out of the Academy.

The robbers didn't drop their guns. *Duh.* Why would they, when it was four against one, including the two monsters?

"Sic 'im," the leader ordered, treating the monsters like they were dogs. Obediently the monsters left their post by the door and approached the dumb cop, circling in from either side.

"Stay back!"

His gun wavering from one target to the other, the cop seemed to realize he'd messed up. He should've just stayed on the floor until the robbery was over, and gone on with his life. But no, he had to do the stupidest thing in the world he could possibly do, and try to be the hero. Now he had two guns aimed at him, and two monsters about to tear him to shreds.

So the cop did the only thing he could do—he started shooting at his attackers. Most of his shots went wild, and monsters were notoriously hard to kill—everybody knew that. Well, maybe everybody except the cop. The few bullets that hit home didn't kill them—it just made them crazier. All hell broke loose. Roaring like berserkers, they started picking up people and tossing them around the room like they were dolls made of straw.

Selina ducked behind a desk and watched, keeping a wary eye on her business associates. More people were screaming and trying to run out of the bank, but she wasn't going to take that chance. Too much carnage between her and the door.

Meanwhile, the two masked men tried to shoot the cop, but hit innocent bystanders, instead. A bullet went through a guy's chest and came out through a bigger hole on the other side. There was lots of blood and gore, which made everyone even more frantic. Finally, the cop was out of bullets. The seven-foot-tall monster grabbed him by the arms, picked him up, and held him over his head.

"No, please," the cop begged. "I'm sorry, I won't… I have a wife!"

The monster flung the cop headfirst through the front window of the bank. The impact shattered the glass, and he landed with a sickening *thud* on the sidewalk. Instantly a pool of blood appeared and began to spread.

While the monsters were distracted by their prey, the people in the bank who weren't dead or injured tried to escape to the street. They pushed through the door and stepped through the shattered window. The monsters grabbed some of them, and Selina saw the dog guy bite a chunk off of some guy's face.

That was enough.

A thousand bucks wasn't worth getting eaten by a monster.

Scooting beneath the teller windows, she reached the door and headed toward the back of the bank. Away from the violence she saw the masked guy with the gravelly voice, carrying a duffel bag filled with money. He approached the leader, and she purposely headed in the other direction.

Selina went to the back, found an exit. Out in the alleyway she crouched, then leaped onto the fire escape. Moments later she was on the roof and sprinting for the front of the building. Looking down toward the street, she saw the masked guys and the monsters getting into the van. The engine revved, and the van peeled away.

Looking off into the distance she saw that, a few blocks away, a bunch of police cars were speeding toward the bank, sirens blaring.

Time to get out of here. Selina jumped onto the next roof, then the next one after that. Within a few short minutes she was ten blocks away. Dropping to the ground in an alleyway, she sauntered out onto the street as another cop car sped past.

Just another teenage street kid in Gotham, looking for her next score.

TWO

"That enough for you tonight, pal?" Jim Gordon glared down at Ricardo DeMonti, the thug whose nose he'd just pulped.

Ricardo spat at Gordon's face, getting him right between the eyes. Gordon grimaced and wiped off the spit, giving his opponent a half-smile.

"I'll take that as a no."

He unloaded a barrage of punches, hearing Ricardo's jawbone crunch, along with some other parts of his face. Gordon didn't particularly enjoy beating the living crap out of people but, yeah, okay, a part of him had missed it. Mainly because it reminded him of what it felt like to be a cop.

It had been five months since Hugo Strange's monsters had swarmed Gotham and Gordon had exited the GCPD for good. He'd just been trying to honor his promise to Bruce Wayne and solve the mystery of who'd killed his parents—give the kid some closure so he could go on with his life and worry about school and running Wayne Enterprises and not solving murder mysteries.

The investigations had led him into Hugo Strange's basement of horrors at Arkham Asylum. Gordon himself had been tortured by Strange, who'd messed with his brain, forced him to give up secrets, and created a psychotic lookalike, Basil, who'd impersonated Gordon for a while. Thank God the doppelganger was off the board, but Gordon felt as if he'd been to hell and hadn't come back yet. He didn't just need a fresh start, he needed a complete reboot, and that meant undoing the biggest mistake of his past.

He'd thought to go down south, start a new life with Leslie Thompkins. She'd had a good reason to dump him when he'd been arrested for murdering Theo Galavan, the mayor of Gotham City. With the Hugo Strange affair behind him, Gordon had planned to beg her forgiveness, do whatever it took to win her back.

His hopes were crushed when he saw her kissing another man.

Gordon didn't know why he'd been surprised. It was the story of his life—*good guy tries to do good, screws up, and has to pick up the pieces*. It wasn't exactly the plot of a romantic comedy. More like a romantic tragedy, really. Gordon had dedicated himself to the GCPD, to cleaning up Gotham, but his career had led to losing his greatest chance at true love.

Nothing was worse than emotional pain. He knew that for a fact. As a police detective Gordon had taken a lot of blows, been pounded on so many times it was a miracle any of his bones were still intact. But while physical injuries would heal, emotional injuries stuck with him for a long, long time—perhaps forever.

Lee hadn't been his first love—there had been others, like Barbara Kean just a couple years ago. Barbara was full-blown psycho though, driven to homicidal madness by the serial killer Jason Skolimski. Harvey Bullock, Gordon's former partner and Gotham's current police captain, had said it best.

"You didn't just dodge a bullet, my man," he'd said, *"you dodged a nuclear freakin' warhead."*

Without a doubt, Barbara had been a huge mistake. He couldn't blame himself though. Charming psychos all wore masks, and Barbara Kean's was drop-dead gorgeous. There had been a time when Gordon had fallen for the mask—not exactly the first guy in history to make that kind of mistake.

Lee, on the other hand, was his soul mate, the woman with whom he'd intended on spending the rest of his life. Keyword "intended." He couldn't blame Lee for taking off. After all, he had been a convicted killer—sent to Blackgate for murder. The fact that Theo Galavan had killed countless people didn't change a thing. Gordon had still killed an unarmed man, shot him in cold blood. While he'd gotten out of Blackgate, in part thanks to Edward Nygma, Gordon would still have to live with his demons—and the knowledge that his actions had cost him the woman he loved.

When he returned to Gotham, he had no job, nowhere to go. He could've crashed at Harvey's place, but he'd put the poor guy through so much already, he wanted to give him a break. Besides, Bullock had his hands full with running the GCPD and catching the monsters. So Gordon rented a cheap basement apartment in the North Village and began the painful search for a job.

Then, ironically, the monster crisis turned into a windfall.

Even with Harvey Bullock as the acting captain, and doing a damned fine job, the GCPD cops couldn't handle the crisis alone—not without help. Mayor Aubrey James announced that there would be bounties paid for any of the monsters brought in, dead or alive. With substantial figures being tossed around, competition for the bounties would be fierce, yet Gordon saw this as the perfect opportunity. Between the skills he'd developed on the force and his contacts in the department, he was confident he could out-hunt any competitor.

So Gordon became a virtual one-man monster-hunting machine. Though he'd had to do things that didn't make him proud, he'd always considered himself to be a moral person, yet he had no qualms about killing these creatures. True, he'd never imagined becoming a bounty hunter, working *outside* of the law, but there were plenty of people in Gotham who wound up doing things they'd never intended to do. Hookers, robbers, killers, monsters—he'd never thought he'd join the list, but circumstances had forced him to evolve.

He was doing it for the money now, and not just

to help society, which felt off. Not because he was his own boss—he loved that part of it—but because he wasn't a public servant to the people of Gotham. He still felt it inside him though—that need to help others would never fade, no matter what job title he claimed.

As a cop Gordon had wanted to clean up Gotham. He wanted to be "that guy" who stood up to the crime bosses and brought peace to Gotham. If peace was even possible in a cesspool like this city. Lately, with maniacs like Penguin and Nygma making their marks on the criminal underworld, Gordon had a sick feeling inside that the worst was yet to come.

Bounty hunting wouldn't be a permanent career, either. Once all the escapees were off the board, he'd move onto something else, but for now there were monsters stalking the streets of his city. Some of the creatures looked like normal people—these were harder to track down, because they'd integrated themselves into society. Thanks to Hugo Strange, others wore ugly deformities that couldn't be hidden, including animalistic features like claws, fangs, and even wings. Many of them, whether young or old, were stronger and faster than normal humans. Their creators had twisted them to have bizarre, inhuman abilities, and no two were alike.

There was only one thing the monsters had in common—they were psychotic. As far as he had seen, they had no remorse, no empathy, no human feelings whatsoever.

In this Strange had deviated from his earlier

experiments, like Karen Jennings. Originally his victims had retained relatively "normal" personalities, but it wasn't the same for this current batch. In a megalomaniacal twist he had given most of them "personas." One example had been Basil, the carbon copy of Gordon himself, a freak with a plastic face, who could alter his appearance and who had almost killed Bullock and a bunch of other cops.

What could Strange's endgame have been? Was he trying to create an army of monsters? Had he gone so far around the bend that he thought he was a god? Strange was in the lockup now, but as far as Gordon knew, he hadn't said a word about his monster experiments. He might take his secrets to the grave.

Tonight's target was a monster ironically named "Nip." Since escaping from Arkham the way most of them had—in the bus Fish Mooney had stolen—Nip had committed numerous robberies and murders, working with a gang of monsters operating on the South Side. His most frequent partner in crime was a female escapee who went by "Tuck."

Cute.

Word on the street was that Ricardo—the guy Gordon was "questioning"—knew where Nip was hiding out. It was hard to feel bad about giving Ricardo a beating. Not exactly one of the good guys, Ricardo had a long rap sheet. Most recently he'd served time at Blackgate for trying to run over his pregnant girlfriend.

Blackgate was where Gordon met Ricardo, when he was there for the murder of Theo Galavan. Ricardo was one of the many inmates who'd taken exception to having an ex-cop around and assaulted Gordon, or *tried* to assault him. Gordon wasn't looking for revenge—he was looking for information. That made it a "win-win" situation.

"One more time," Gordon said. "Where's Nip?"

"I already told you, I don't know." When he spoke something rattled in his voice, but Gordon got the essence of it.

"You made a payment to him last week."

"I make payments to a lot of people," Ricardo said. "That's what I do—I'm like a messenger, but I don't ask questions and I don't know who I'm dealing with. I swear."

"You don't know when you deal with a monster?"

"Some of 'em look real," Ricardo protested. "I mean, like people. You think I'm gonna deal with a monster on purpose? You think I'm crazy?"

Gordon pressed the gun into Ricardo's neck.

"You can't kill me," Ricardo said. "You're a cop."

"*Was* a cop," Gordon said. "Now I can do whatever the hell I want."

"Still..." Ricardo said. "I mean you wouldn't actually... *Madre de Dios*, man, that'd be *murder*."

In fact, killing scum like Ricardo shouldn't exactly cause Gordon to lose sleep.

Gordon had done a lot of things he wouldn't have expected to do, especially since coming back to Gotham.

This wasn't going to be one of them—though there was no way Ricardo could know that. Gordon just grinned.

"Things change," he said. "So let me make a suggestion." He pushed the gun deeper into Ricardo's neck, hard enough that it would make breathing difficult and incite some healthy panic. "Don't test me."

"Oh… Okay." Ricardo was barely able to speak.

"You've got five seconds before your body becomes rat food." Gordon nodded off to the left. Nearby a few of the rodents were devouring a dead pigeon, perfectly emphasizing his point.

"One…"

"Okay, man, but you're crazy lookin' for Nip," Ricardo said. "His teeth are like knives. I hear he bit a guy's hand off."

"Two…" Gordon said. "Three…" One of the rats bit into a bone, causing it to snap.

"Okay, okay—take it easy," Ricardo said quickly, spitting some blood so he could talk. "Nip hangs out in a burnt-down building down by the docks."

That made sense. Monsters gravitated toward abandoned buildings. Especially the inmates who looked like refugees from a freak show and wanted to stay out of the public eye.

"C'mon, Ricky, there's dozens of burnt-out buildings down there," Gordon said. "Be more specific."

"I… I dunno. I only met him there once."

"Your five seconds are up."

"Lamppost!" The thug nearly shouted.

"What the hell does that mean?"

"There's a lamppost, it fell down, guess a car hit it or whatever. Anyway, it's leaning against the building. That's the building where I met Nip."

"When was he there?"

"Few days ago. That's all I know, I swear."

Gordon believed him. They were done here. Before Ricardo figured out what was going on, he'd been cuffed to a drainpipe.

"Hey, what're you doing?" Ricardo said. "I thought you aren't a cop no more."

"I'm not, but I still have this problem I can't shake."

"Problem? What problem's that?"

"I hate scumbag thugs like you."

"C'mon, man, I did what you wanted," the thug protested, then he spit out some more blood. "I gave you the info you asked for, you son of a bitch."

"You violated your parole and there's a warrant out for your arrest," Gordon said. "You see, I do my research." He turned to walk out of the alleyway.

"Hey, where're you going?" Ricardo yelled, his voice going high. "You can't leave me here! Hey, come back! Hey!"

Reaching the street, Gordon opened his flip phone and called Harvey Bullock.

"Jimmy, my man," Bullock said. "Got another monster for us?"

"Not at the moment," Gordon said, "but I got a bad human." He described the location where he'd left Ricardo.

"We'll pick him up as soon as possible," Bullock said. "Like maybe tomorrow morning. I like to let the bad guys fester a little, contemplate their sins, so to speak."

"Who's more compassionate than you?"

"Nobody," Bullock said. "I put the passion in compassionate."

Gordon laughed.

"We need to hang sometime," Bullock suggested. "Wanna get a brewsky later?"

"Can't tonight. I have plans."

"Yeah? A hot date, you dog?"

"Guess you can say that," Gordon replied. He never told anyone when he had a lead. If the cops got to Nip first, he wouldn't get his bounty.

"Look at you," Bullock said, blissfully ignorant. "You can knock Jim Gordon out of the game, but you can't keep him on the sidelines. Seriously, way to rebound, my man. Lee's an amazing woman, don't get me wrong, but there's a lot of other amazing women out there. Take it from me—I've been dumped by most of them. You just gotta make sure the femme fatales don't bite you on the ass on their way out the door. I mean, if you get my drift."

"I'll be in touch," Gordon said, reaching his car and getting in.

"Yeah, lemme know how it goes tonight," Bullock said. "I want the play-by-play, brother."

"You know me," Gordon said. "I don't kill and tell."

"Excuse me?"

Gordon ended the call.

THREE

"Kill and tell?" Bullock said. His visitor shot him a curious look. "The hell's he talking about? He means that as a figure of speech, right?"

Now that Bullock was the captain of the GCPD, he had the big upstairs office. This was one chair he'd never thought his fat Irish ass would be sitting in. Lucius Fox, who'd been hired for Edward Nygma's old job in forensics, had just come in to update him on a couple of cases that were in progress.

"I'm no mind reader," Fox said, "but, given Jim's history as a straight shooter, I'd hazard a guess that he's planning to kill someone."

"Someone or some*thing*," Bullock said. "After all, Jim's turned out to be the best damn monster hunter in Gotham. At the rate he's going, he's gonna make us all look bad, if we don't step up our game."

"Nobody's blaming you for the monster problem, Harvey. That's on Hugo Strange—and, I suppose, Thomas Wayne if you want to connect all the dots."

"Yeah, well, I'm one of those dots," Bullock said. "A big fat dot that didn't catch on to Strange fast enough. It's worse now that the whole shebang is my responsibility. You read the papers? Every time a monster robs somebody, or kills somebody, the smart-ass reporters talk about what a half-assed job the GCPD's doing, like they expect me to push a button and boom, problem's solved. 'A disgrace to his profession'—that's how they see me, and it's a direct quote from this morning's paper. Not exactly what I want carved into my tombstone. Maybe I should frame it and hang it up next to the diploma I don't have."

"So which monster do you think Jim's after?" Fox asked.

"That's anyone's guess," Bullock replied. "We don't even know for sure how many monsters are still out there, roaming the streets. Ten, twenty, thirty, fifty?"

"Our latest guess is twenty-seven."

"Call me crazy," Bullock said, "but we shouldn't be using the word 'guess' in connection with these… things. Whatever you've got, it can wait. Get me a list of every known monster, cross-referenced with the ones that have been taken out of circulation, and the last known whereabouts of the ones that are left."

He paused, then added, "If Jim's onto a bust, we gotta get him some backup, 'cause you just *know* he'll be too proud to ask for it."

"I'm on it, boss," Fox said, doing an about-face.

Boss. Bullock shook his head.

He had been in charge for five months and that

word—"boss"—still didn't compute. He'd never been in charge of anything before. After all, who in their right mind would let Harvey Bullock be captain of a ship? It'd take a disaster, like hitting an iceberg, for that to happen.

Well, the Arkham monsters had been the iceberg.

Harvey was great at a lot of things, but bossing people around was a challenge for him—especially the kind of bossing a police captain was expected to do. He didn't much like being the recipient of the bossing, either—well, unless he was getting a little side action on the weekends from his favorite dominatrix.

While he'd been doing his best to run the show, even enjoying the rush at times, it wasn't usually Bullock's style to be the point man. He liked being in the background, the number two or—better yet—number three in command, because then when you messed up, no one gave a rat's ass. As *numero uno*, however, the fate of GCPD was in Harvey Bullock's hands. Sometimes that scared the shit out of him.

Still, he was up for a challenge. He'd been working his Irish ass off, trying to be the best police captain he could be. The promotion should've been a great achievement, a terrific career move, and something to be proud of. It still could be. Though the pressure dampened his spirits, he relished the opportunity to prove himself.

When news first broke about Bullock's promotion, everybody congratulated him like he'd just won the freakin' lottery.

"Congrats for what?" Bullock would quip. "I get double the work, but the same pay. Yeah, lucky me." It wasn't like he'd had a choice though. Barnes was still in the hospital, and there was no telling when he'd get out. Someone had to step up to the plate, and fate had tapped Harvey Bullock.

Fate has a helluva sick sense of humor, he mused.

Used to be Bullock could imagine Jim Gordon as the captain someday, but the poor bastard had chased after his woman, and look what it got him. Harvey loved Jim like a brother, and was always supportive, but did he think Jim had a chance of getting Lee back?

No, sirree, he thought. *When a woman leaves you and you chase 'em, you're just looking for another kick in the ass.* If Jim really wanted to get his woman back, the best thing he could do was ignore the crap out of them. How'd the saying go? *"If you love a bird, you let it fly away, and if it loves you too, it flies back."* Some bullshit like that.

In Harvey's experience, very few he'd let go had ever flown back, nor had he wanted them to. Regardless, the adage still made sense.

Jim Gordon hadn't listened, and now he was beyond reasoning. Poor guy had done a stint at Blackgate, got his brain messed with by Hugo Strange, and then dumped—for a second time, no less. It was a tough trifecta.

There's an easy way to avoid rejection, he thought. *Don't get involved in the first place.* Keep it light, keep it fun, keep it simple. Those were Harvey's mottos. Okay, he wasn't exactly proud of his "romantic life," but he wasn't ashamed either. He didn't like sugarcoating himself, or leading anybody on. He made it clear from the get-go that he was a shallow shell of a man, incapable of maintaining a healthy relationship with anyone, including himself. That way nobody got hurt.

"Enough with the philosophy bullshit," he said to no one in particular. "It's time to kick some monster butt."

"The more of them we capture or kill, the harder it gets to find the rest as they go to ground," Lucius Fox said, turning away from the tactical map. "Our best bet—"

Suddenly a uniform—Officer Reynolds, Bullock thought—came rushing through the door, interrupting the meeting.

"There's been a new incident."

"Monsters?" Bullock asked.

"Sounds like it," Reynolds said.

"Okay," Bullock announced, standing to face the assemblage. "This meeting's officially adjourned." Truth be told it was his favorite thing about meetings—adjourning them. "So what've we got?" he asked Reynolds.

"Gotham Savings. Armed robbery. Officer Down. Civilian fatalities, lots of injuries. From what I hear, it's a bloodbath."

"Mother of God in heaven," Bullock said.

"Who do you want on the case?" Reynolds asked.

"I'm taking this one myself."

"But you're the Captain," Reynolds said.

"Yeah, and that means I'm the boss, which means I

can tell myself what to do." He felt pretty good saying it too. Maybe the job was growing on him. "Collins, tag along," he added, gesturing toward a kid who still looked wet behind the ears. Rick Collins was a young detective who'd recently been promoted, all crisp and clean in his new suit. It looked like he was excited, getting to work with the big boss. It was like a rookie getting called up from the minors and batting cleanup in his first game.

Poor chump, Bullock thought.

"Yes, sir, Mr. Bullock," Collins said.

"Whoa, no need for misters or sirs," Bullock said. "You gonna work with me, we're gonna keep it on a half-name basis. Call me Harv."

Driving to a crime scene without Jim Gordon still felt weird to Bullock. It just felt unnatural to not have his buddy next to him. Yeah, he had worked solo during Gordon's stretch at Blackgate, but Jim had been Bullock's only real partner since Angela, God rest her. She'd had a mouth on her, knew how to dish it out but, yeah, okay, Harvey had loved her.

It took a lot for Harvey to love somebody, and the violent way she'd checked out hadn't made it any easier. Whenever he thought about her it reminded him of why he didn't play the love game to begin with. He had enough pain in his life and didn't need to bring a woman into the mix. It wasn't that he was sexist—in fact, it was the total opposite. He loved women, but avoided getting involved with them for their own good, as a freakin' public service.

No woman deserved Harvey Bullock as a partner, for damn sure.

"So, um, what do you want me to do when we get there?" Collins asked.

Poor kid. He looked cool on the outside, but was probably sweating on the inside like a basketball player in the fourth quarter.

"Don't worry about it, rookie," Bullock said, "just follow my lead."

A few minutes later they pulled up in front of the bank, triple-parking next to all the squad cars and ambulances. The front window to the bank was smashed, and there was blood all over the sidewalk. Emergency medical workers were carrying out a few bodies. Unfortunately, the scene had become typical lately. It seemed like every day there was some new monster-related violence in Gotham. Sometimes Bullock wondered if the city would be better off if Hugo Strange had just set off the nuke.

They got out of the car and headed toward the entrance. The revolving doors were folded back, and an officer lifted the crime scene tape so Bullock and Collins could pass under it.

"Okay, let's see what we got," Bullock said.

Even more than out on the sidewalk, there was blood everywhere—on the floor, the desk, the tellers' windows. Even, somehow, the ceiling.

"I'm impressed."

"With what?" Collins asked. He was surprisingly calm, staring at a blood puddle.

"Your stomach, for one," Bullock replied. "A lot of rookies would be puking up their guts right about now."

"I like blood," Collins said.

Bullock gave the kid a double take. *Okay, that sounded a little wacky. I hope we don't have another Edward Nygma on our hands.*

Officer Louis Rojas came over.

"Hey, Louie," Bullock said. "What do we got?"

"Nightmare," Rojas said. "Six down including Officer Hunt."

"Jesus wept... Was he responding?"

"No, off duty."

"Tried to play superhero, I guess," Bullock said. "Good on him for trying though. We need more heroes in Gotham." As he listened to himself talk, Harvey had to admit he was kind of impressed. He actually sounded like a leader, saying all the right things. Not long ago he hadn't even known this side of him existed.

"You got that right," Rojas said. "The situation could get even worse though. We got three people headed to the hospital in critical condition. Good news is we found the guard."

"*Found* him?"

"He was grabbed at the start of the robbery, thrown into the van. Found him about ten minutes ago, in a ditch off the expressway. A few broken bones, but he'll live."

"We get a description of the getaway vehicle?"

"Yeah, but we already recovered it, not far from the ditch. So they either switched cars or somebody picked them up."

"What about the crew?" Bullock asked. "Who're we dealing with here?"

"Witnesses say there were four guys," Rojas said. "Well, two guys and two monsters. The men were in masks. One had a deep voice—a couple of people said he seemed to be the leader."

"Great," Bullock said. "Let's get to the opera house. Maybe if we arrest every baritone in Gotham, we'll find our guy."

"What about the monsters?" Collins asked.

"One was big, like seven feet. Had multi-colored skin."

"Multi-colored skin?" Bullock said. "The hell does that mean?"

"Like blue. Green. Maybe some other colors mixed in."

"Sounds like a real catch for a lucky lady."

"Do monsters have girlfriends?" Rojas asked.

"Some do, some don't," Bullock said. "Just like single cops. We ain't so different. Any video?"

"No, the video security system wasn't working, for some reason."

"Yeah, that sounds like a real coincidence," Bullock said sarcastically. "Let's look into what happened with that, and pronto."

"What about the other monster?" Collins asked. Rojas shot him a scowl.

"Shorter, not multi-colored, didn't talk at all."

"Probably doesn't know how to talk," Bullock said. "Strange made some of them mute."

"I think these monsters have priors," Collins said.

"Yeah?" Bullock replied. "And how do you know that, rookie? You got a crystal ball? Tea leaves?"

"They fit the description of two who escaped the scene of a liquor store robbery on Blanchard, off Finley, a couple of months ago."

"I remember that case," Bullock said. "It wasn't monster-related."

"One witness, Daniella Curtis, reported two monsters leaving the scene. Detectives discredited her account because she's a junkie, but it's probably worth talking to her. Maybe these monsters are part of the same crew that robbed the liquor store, or there's a connection that could tell us more."

Rojas's scowl was replaced by an impressed look. Bullock, on the other hand, was as annoyed as hell. Last thing in the world he needed was another know-it-all partner.

"Let's not waste our time rummaging through the cold case files, all right?" he growled. "Stay in the present tense, and that means talking to all the witnesses here, getting their accounts."

Collins didn't move.

"Like *now*," Bullock said.

Collins hesitated a moment longer. "Right, sir," he said, and he walked away to where a couple of witnesses were talking to a beat cop. Sometimes

Bullock hated this giving-out-orders crap. This wasn't one of those times. He smiled with satisfaction as the rookie snapped to it.

"As bad as this looks," Rojas said, interrupting the moment, "it could've been much worse. The monsters were tearing up the place—people included. Luckily, the whole crew took off when they heard the sirens."

"What was the take?" Harvey asked.

"About two hundred grand according to the bank manager." Rojas glanced to his right. Bullock followed his gaze and saw a conservative-looking woman in a blue dress, her hair in a bun. "Her name's Clarissa Morgan."

"Let's get the names and phone numbers of every employee," Bullock instructed. "I want to know why the security video wasn't operational. There might've been someone working on the inside."

Hearing his voice, Morgan glanced in Bullock's direction. It seemed like maybe she recognized him, although he'd have sworn he'd never seen her before.

Must've caught me on TV.

"There's one witness we haven't been able to talk to yet," Rojas said. "A teenage girl. Just before all hell broke loose, she approached the guard and said there was something happening outside. When the guard went to check it out, that's when he got kidnapped."

"Now that *is* interesting," Bullock said. "So where is this girl?"

"Your guess is as good as mine. People said she was in the bank one second, gone the next."

"Do we know what she looked like?"

"Pretty, short curly hair, black leather jacket."

Uh-oh, Bullock thought. Half-smiling, he said, "Figures."

"What figures?"

"Let's just say I'm pretty sure I know who that is, and it's not a surprise to find her in the middle of trouble. Make that one hundred percent." That got him moving. "Later, Louie." Stepping quickly over to Collins, he said, "C'mon, kid, let's go. We should be able to break this case by sundown."

Minutes later they were speeding away in the car. Now that they were alone again, Bullock felt the need to impart some wisdom to the rookie.

"If you want to work with me, Collins, there's one rule you have to never forget—you gotta be careful to not make your boss look stupid. There's a term for that, and it's 'career suicide.'"

"I didn't mean any disrespect, Mr. Bullock," Collins replied. "I mean Harv." Bullock couldn't tell if he meant it. At least he *sounded* sincere.

"Don't sweat it," Bullock said. "So you still want to work with me, huh?"

"Of course, why wouldn't I?"

"'Cause you should realize that by working with me, you're taking a big risk."

"A risk?"

"Yeah, a risk. You like taking risks?"

"Um, yeah," Collins said. "I mean, I guess."

Harvey made a sharp left, tires squealing. "I'm not talking about risks like playing the daily double at the racetrack. I'm talking about serious life-and-death-type risks. Like we're talking Russian roulette level, where you make one wrong move and that's it, *poof*, the whole shebang goes up in flames."

"I'm not following."

"Just like all my ex-girlfriends, all my old partners are either dead, went nuts, or did jail time." He paused to let that sink in. "You still like your odds?"

"I'm sure I can handle it." Collins didn't seem at all rattled. Hard to tell if it was a good thing, or bad.

"Confidence is good," Bullock said. "Cockiness? Not so much. It can get you killed." He was enjoying busting the kid's chops. "So you really think you're a risk taker, huh?"

"Um, yeah…" Collins replied. "I mean, I, um, yes."

"What kind of risks do you like to take?"

"Uh… I um…"

"Do you climb mountains? Jump out of planes? Jaywalk?"

"What?"

"Like when there's heavy traffic in midtown Gotham. Trucks, buses. Would you just walk into the middle of it like you got your head up your ass, like your life doesn't matter?"

"No, sir."

"Good answer. A woman I once dated gave me crap 'cause I didn't jaywalk with her one time—said I didn't have the guts. Can you believe it?" He put one hand on his chest, fingers splayed. "Me? Harvey Bullock, a guy who puts his life on the line every day for this city. I'm not a risk taker?" He was getting off track. "My point is, there are smart risks in life, and stupid risks. If you understand the difference you'll go places, kid."

"What happened to the woman?" Collins asked.

"What do you think?" Bullock said. "Got run over by a speeding laundry truck. Forty-seven years old, had half her life ahead of her. Miss Risktaker's six feet under now, pushing up daises."

Bullock hung a right.

"Sorry," he said with a smirk. "I know that was a little risky."

"Where we heading?" Collins asked.

"To try to find a girl named Selina Kyle."

"What for?"

"Leave that to me," Bullock said. "You just worry about staying alive, kid."

FOUR

Selina Kyle had some time to kill before she had to show at the meeting spot, but she didn't feel like going home. Maybe if she'd had a home, she'd feel like going to it, but when "home" was a flophouse for street kids, she tried to stay away from it as much as she could.

Walking past a bar in the South Village, Selina spotted a rich-looking guy.

She didn't even have to think about it.

The guy wore a fancy suit, had a fat wallet in his back pocket, and best of all, he was so sloshed he could barely walk, stumbling and even grabbing onto railings and random people. Robbing drunk people was the easiest money. If some rich idiot wanted to go around Gotham at night, with monsters loose in the city and a fat wallet in his back pocket, he was practically begging to get robbed.

If Selina didn't do it, somebody else definitely would.

When she came up behind him, she spotted his expensive gold watch. Better and better. She could pawn the watch easy downtown, but still she figured she'd go for his wallet first, make it look like she'd bumped into him by accident. Usually that wasn't the best way because sometimes the mark got suspicious, but this guy was so drunk she could probably say, *Hey, loser, gimme your money*, and he'd probably just hand his wallet to her.

Then, after she bumped into him she'd ask for directions, act like she was some dumb, scared, lost tourist or something. It'd be like, *Excuse me, mister, but how do I get to the Gotham Plaza Hotel?* As he gave her directions, she'd slip the watch off his wrist. She'd stolen watches from sober guys, so this wouldn't take any effort at all.

Before she took off, she'd say, *Thank you, mister*, and he'd answer, *You're welcome*. That was the best part—hearing the people she'd robbed say, *You're welcome*, like they'd done *her* a favor. They *had* done her a favor, of course—just not the favor they'd thought.

Selina was a few inches behind him, so close she could smell his gross perfume, when he turned into Lenny's Pool Hall.

A pool hall? Seriously?

The best places to pick pockets were in big crowds or on dark, empty streets. A pool hall was neither. Normally she would've bailed and found another mark, but she really wanted that watch. Besides, what else was she going to do till the meet-up? It wasn't like Prince Charming—or even Bruce Wayne—was waiting for her at a ball.

Bruce Wayne.

Selina had gone the whole day without thinking about him, but now he popped into her head again. She'd never admit this to anyone—sometimes she didn't even admit it to herself—but she liked him. Well, more than liked him. There was just something that made him different. It definitely wasn't coolness. No, Bruce Wayne was *not* cool. He wasn't a dork, either, although he probably should've been a dork, given how he'd been raised.

Bruce had fascinated her since the first time she saw him, the night his parents were killed, and somehow that fascination may have developed into something more. It was weird because, although they had nothing in common, it felt like they had *everything* in common. She hadn't seen him in months, not since Hugo Strange's monsters had escaped from Arkham. She'd heard that his butler, Alfred, had whisked him away to Switzerland, which was such an Alfred thing to do.

Whenever there was danger, Alfred acted like he had to protect Bruce, like the kid was made of glass or something. What was up with that?

Maybe Bruce didn't have a choice, she thought. *Maybe the trip had already been planned*. She hoped so, 'cause running away just because some monsters had gotten loose still seemed like a wimpy thing to do.

That reminded her of the bank, and she suppressed a shudder.

It's still *a wimpy thing to do…*

Honestly, Selina didn't know how she felt about

Bruce. Sometimes she thought he was just a stuck-up rich kid, but then he'd show his cool, brave side and she'd think, *Maybe this guy has potential after all*. Still, he had a lot of growing up to do. Although they were both sixteen years old, Selina felt way more mature than him.

He could be surprising though, like coming to live with her on the streets. She'd seen him get beaten up a few times too. On the surface he was a spoiled rich kid, but he didn't act like it. Maybe that's what she liked most about Bruce, that he kept her guessing. Some people were so square—once you met them you knew exactly where they were—but Bruce was more like a puzzle that seemed impossible to solve.

He was kind of cute too, but she would never tell him that. It'd go straight to his head. No, she was wasting her time even thinking about him. More likely Bruce Wayne *was* just a spoiled rich kid. And the cool, brave side that she'd thought she'd seen? It didn't exist.

As she turned to enter the pool hall, a big hairy paw grabbed her. For a split second she actually panicked.

It's a monster!

When her arm wasn't ripped off she looked over and took a deep breath. Yeah, it was a gorilla, but the human kind.

"No kids allowed."

Selina yanked her arm free. "Says who?"

"Says the law." He leaned in close. "Says *me*."

"Yeah, like you, or anybody else in Gotham ever pays any attention to the law." To her surprise the guy sort of nodded, realizing Selina had a good point. Then he crossed his arms.

"Well, law or no law, I'm not letting you in."

"Then how come *he's* in here?" Selina gestured toward a guy who seemed to be about her age. The kid was shooting pool, making a hard combination shot. Everybody standing around cheered for him.

The gorilla shot her a frown, but he gave it up.

"A'right, go in. But keep your nose clean." Whatever that meant.

"Thanks, big guy." Selina headed over to the bar, hopped onto a stool, and looked around the room for her mark. It was crowded and noisy.

"Hey, kid," the bartender said. "If you're gonna hang out here, you gotta buy something."

"Gimme a scotch on the rocks."

The guy crossed his hands in front of his chest.

"It was a joke," Selina said. "How 'bout Coke? Am I old enough for that?" The bartender uncrossed his arms and reached for the nozzle and a glass.

"Hey, long time no see."

She jumped a little. It was the kid who'd made the pool shot. Selina hadn't recognized him before, but now he seemed familiar.

"It's me, Johnny," he said. "Remember?"

Oh, right. He hung out with a gang by the railroad tracks uptown. Even Selina had to admit Johnny was kind of cute. Short spiky dark hair, blue eyes, dimples.

"Yeah, I know who you are," Selina said, not letting her thought show.

"You like that shot I made?"

"What shot?"

"I saw you watching."

"Oh, *that* shot. Yeah, it was okay."

Selina's soda arrived. She took a sip, pretending she hoped Johnny would walk away, but she really didn't want him to leave. She liked the attention, even from wise-asses. As she sipped, she saw her mark in the corner, sitting on a bench.

Bingo.

"Where's your boyfriend?"

She frowned. "I don't have a boyfriend."

"Yeah? So you and Bruce Wayne broke up?"

Selina shot him a look. She hated that people were talking about her and Bruce like that. What, was this *high school*? Or what she imagined high school would be like, if she'd ever gone. People in each other's business, creating drama.

"We were never together," Selina said.

"Yeah? So that's how you roll, huh?"

"What do you mean?" She knew exactly what he meant, but now she was pissed off. She wanted him to make more of an idiot out of himself. It'd be fun to watch.

"I mean it sounds like you don't get too attached, which I'm totally cool with." He rested a hand on her shoulder.

Selina kneed him in the groin.

Johnny doubled over, coughing, trying to catch his breath. A couple of guys near the pool table saw what happened and laughed.

"Ouch," one of them said.

"Looks like that's strike three, Johnny," another added.

They laughed harder.

"Y-y-you're gonna pay for that," Johnny said to Selina.

"Oooh, I'm so scared," she replied. "Look at me, I'm trembling."

Selina noticed that the drunk guy was gone.

"Oh, man," she said. Pushing past Johnny she went to the back of the hall, beyond the pool tables. There were no women in the place—just gross-looking guy after gross-looking guy. She felt like she was walking through Blackgate prison. It began to creep her out, and it took *a lot* to creep Selina out.

Then she saw the drunk guy heading toward the bathroom. Rushing up from behind, she bumped into him.

"Oops, sorry, Mister." The guy turned around all wobbly and gave her a drunken stare.

Selina already had his wallet.

"You know, you look a lot like my uncle," she said. "You don't have a sister who deserted her kid at an orphanage, do you?"

"What?" The guy was practically begging to get robbed.

"Never mind."

She had his watch now. It was too easy. Bored and ready to head for the rendezvous, she pushed through the crowd, heading back to the front and toward the door. A voice cut through the hubbub behind her.

"When you least expect it, expect it." It was Johnny.

"I'm so scared I'm shivering," Selina said, not really expecting him to hear. She felt good, elated the way she did after every successful score. Ducking into the first alley she came to, Selina opened the wallet.

Eleven bucks?

Either she'd completely overestimated the guy, or he'd spent all of his cash on booze. If only she'd spotted him *before* he'd gotten smashed. What the hell, she still had the watch. That should get her a hundred bucks easy at a pawnshop. Still not bad for twenty minutes' work. Exiting the alley, she crossed onto the next street. Glancing around to make sure there were no cops around, she saw something that made her heart jump.

Bruce Wayne.

Clear as day, on a corner across the street. He was there one second, then a car passed by, and he was gone. She rushed over, not waiting for the light to change, dodging traffic. But when she made it to the corner, no one was there.

"Bruce?" she called, looking around.

No answer.

Maybe she'd just imagined it.

"Bruce? Hello?"

Still nothing. She waited for a couple minutes longer, glancing this way and that. Then she shrugged and continued on her way.

Running to keep pace with a bus she jumped onto the back. No one noticed, or if they did they didn't care. After about twenty minutes she hopped off on the other side of Gotham, near Fish Mooney's old club. Selina had been swinging past there regularly, hoping to catch sight of its former owner. It wasn't likely, when you thought about it, but she'd always thought of herself as lucky—certainly more so than the average person. Lucky to have survived childhood, and lucky enough to get out of more than her share of jams.

Strangely enough, Fish seemed to fill a gap in Selina's life. Her mother had taken off when Selina was only five, leaving her at St. Maria's orphanage. That was where she'd begun to develop the skills she needed to survive on her own, and before she was a teenager she moved onto the streets. Overall she was happy on her own, independent and without anyone telling her what to do, but a part of her still wondered what it would be like to have a mom.

"Monster, monster! Turn back, turn back!"

A man, maybe forty, came running around the corner, slipping and almost losing his balance. The guy was waving his arms like a lunatic, and as she ducked to one side he ran past her. Without hesitation she took off at a sprint in the direction from which he'd come, not breaking stride as she turned the corner. Then she skidded to a stop.

There were two dead bodies in the middle of the street, so bloody and smashed up it was hard to tell if they were men or women, or one of each. Judging from the weird way their arms and legs were splayed, they had to have fallen from pretty high up. It looked like they'd committed suicide, but *two* suicides?

That didn't make sense.

Then, from way above, Selina heard a weird roar—like some kind of wild animal. She looked up and saw this huge—well, green *thing*—falling from above, coming straight toward her. With her quick catlike reflexes, Selina leapt backward out of the way, expecting the thing to smash against the pavement like the two dead people. When that happened she'd wind up with blood and guts all over her.

Still, it was better than being dead.

With a *thud* the monster landed on his feet, only a few inches in front of her. This was one of the grotesque monsters, too. It looked like a fat bald guy, but with scaly, bumpy green skin and yellow, slitted eyes, like an alligator. It hissed and glared at her like she was its next meal. She'd seen a lot of psychos— both in Arkham and on the streets—but she'd never seen anything as freaky at this one.

Looking in its eyes felt like looking at pure evil.

Gross.

The monster lunged at her faster than she could react, swinging with its clawed hands, slashing her left arm while knocking her backward onto the pavement. The monster hissed again, exposing its sharp, pointy teeth.

Well, it was nice while it lasted.

As the monster lunged she figured this was it. Unlike the stray cats she liked so much, she didn't have nine lives, or even two.

Her luck had officially run out.

FIVE

Down by the docks, Gordon parked in front of the burnt-out building with a lamppost leaning against it, just as Ricardo had described. He counted seven stories. While it seemed as if he'd been given good info, Gordon wasn't going to take any chances. It could be a setup and, as a habit, he always prepared for the worst.

One major downside to being a bounty hunter was the lack of any backup. It was Gordon vs. the world—or in this case, Gordon vs. the monsters. Sometimes he missed the security of going into a bust, knowing that Harvey or even a whole SWAT team was working with him and could save his ass if he got into a situation where his ass needed saving.

On the other hand, as a private citizen he didn't have to worry as much about police protocol, like he had when he'd killed Galavan and wound up at Blackgate. Now if he needed to shoot to kill, he could do so and only have to worry about god's judgment, not the law's.

Checking his gun and supply of ammo, he exited the car.

There was no way to approach the building without being seen, so he didn't try to hide the fact that he was there. He'd just have to take his chances. Pulling out a flashlight he pushed through the front entrance. The large wooden door had been left ajar, propped open with a cinderblock. Not really surprising. Once they'd been found, monsters didn't tend to care all that much about personal security, probably because they saw themselves as being at the top of the food chain.

"GCPD!" The sound echoed through the cavernous space.

Crap! he thought. *Old habits die hard.*

"Nip, I know you're in here!" he said. "Turn yourself in now, or you're leaving in a bag! The choice is yours!"

Some people might think that taunting a monster wasn't the brightest idea, but Gordon had learned that taking a tough stance with these bastards was the best way to go. It seemed to startle the creatures, throw them off-kilter, which made them easier to take down. Most likely they were used to people running away, so when somebody took the opposite approach, it threw them.

Whatever the reason, it had worked so far.

It wasn't like much research had gone into monster behavior. Gordon doubted if even Hugo Strange, a lunatic himself, had any idea how his creations would act in a given situation. All they seemed to have in common was that they were psychotic and lacked any measurable conscience. It was all a big free-flowing experiment and, unfortunately, the citizens of Gotham had been tagged as the guinea pigs.

He'd heard that Fish Mooney had been responsible for the Arkham breakout. While Gordon had been defusing the bomb that could've turned a huge swath of Gotham into nuclear debris, she'd escaped in a bus that contained dozens of inmates—probably a bus Strange had intended to use for his own getaway.

Everyone had thought that Fish was off the board, but Strange—that sick bastard—had somehow revived her. The monsters she released had wreaked havoc on the city, murdering dozens of innocents.

So far Gordon had single-handedly brought more than a half-dozen of the Arkham escapees to justice. Despite what some people thought of him, Gordon's preference wasn't to kill. He didn't even want to kill monsters, unless forced to do so. That said, sometimes killing them was a better alternative than leaving them on the street, where they could—and would—kill god knows how many innocent citizens.

With the long beam from his flashlight guiding him, Gordon moved slowly through the building. It looked like it might have been some kind of event space, the cavernous main area boasting high ceilings. No matter how nice it might have been in its heyday, now it was dank and dreary with shattered glass and garbage all over the floor. A huge chandelier hung at an angle from the ceiling.

Stopping in the center of the room, Gordon listened for a sign of his quarry—or anyone—but he didn't hear anything. He would have preferred to secure the first floor before heading upstairs, but he didn't have that luxury. Again, he missed having Harvey around for backup. How many times had Bullock saved his life in situations like these? Too many to count.

"Nip, you in here?" he called out. "If you are, come out now with your hands up, or else!" There was a strong possibility that he was wasting his breath. Monsters rarely gave themselves up—especially not the stronger ones. They rarely ran away, either. While they tried to remain out of sight, they would fight viciously when cornered, leading to three possible outcomes: kill, be killed, or get captured.

"Nip, let's just make this easier for both of us!" he said. "You know we're going to fight this out eventually, *hombre a hombre*, so how 'bout we just cut to the chase so one of us can get on with his life?"

Gordon liked to talk tough when he was hunting monsters. It gave him at least an illusion of control. Often it really *was* a waste of his breath though. One monster had been stone cold deaf. In fact, some of them didn't have any ears at all.

Nip had been photographed though, and he had ears—four of them. There was no telling how this affected his hearing. Hugo Strange might have created a four-eared monster to test a theory, or as a perverse private joke. When it came to depravity, Strange seemed to have no limits. Other than the ears, however, Nip looked pretty much normal.

"How'd you find me?"

Gordon tensed. He couldn't tell where the voice had come from. Above him? Behind him? The acoustics were distorted, maybe because the place was so huge.

"Nip, is that you?"

"Yeah, it's me."

It sounded like the voice had come from above. It was a normal, working-class Gotham accent, but that didn't mean he was normal. Gordon's clay-faced doppelganger had sounded normal too, but in the end he'd proved to be a raging psycho. Unfortunately, he was still out there somewhere.

"I'm not here to hurt you unless you try to hurt me," Gordon said. "I'm here to help you get the help you desperately need. Trust me, letting me take you in peacefully is your best option right now."

"You really expect me to fall for that crap?"

Now the voice sounded like it had come from behind. Why did he feel as if he was trapped in the house of mirrors at the Gotham Fair? Gordon wheeled around, shining his flashlight, but he didn't see anyone there.

"How'd you know my name?"

Nip's hearty laugh echoed. "Every monster in Gotham knows who Jim Gordon is. You're worse than the cops. Bet you didn't know there's a bounty on *your* head, which goes to the guy who takes you out, did you?"

Nip was above him again. Gordon turned the flashlight upward, illuminating the crystals of the chandelier that hung from the rafters.

"Yeah?" Gordon said. "So who put out this bounty?"

"You mean who are we gonna collect from?"

We?

Gordon didn't like the sound of that.

It came from his left this time, and he turned the beam in that direction. He couldn't see anyone there, but he did spot a light switch. Moving quickly over, hoping the power was still on, he flicked the switch. The chandelier lit up and the sudden brightness was practically blinding.

"Nip!" Gordon called out, but he could hardly see anything. Then he heard two gunshots in quick succession, and his flashlight was knocked out of his hand, followed instantly by his gun. As his eyes adjusted to the brightness, he saw what appeared to be a man.

Aside from the deformity of having four ears, Nip looked very much human. He was clean-cut and even handsome, wearing a vintage navy suit, dark shirt, white tie and a white fedora. He was holding the gun he had fired.

"Nice way to introduce yourself," Gordon said.

"Under the circumstances I think it was appropriate," Nip said. "Oh, and I apologize in advance for having to kill you." He smiled, showing off his very sharp, dog-like teeth, just as Ricardo had described. From about ten feet away he aimed the gun at Gordon's head.

"Hold it," Gordon said. "If you're serious about this bounty on me, aren't I worth more alive?

"No, actually you're worth more dead. Quite a bit more. Someone is hell-bent on getting rid of you. And since you've killed or arrested many of my... friends,

I have personal reasons for enjoying this moment. So, please, excuse me while I revel in it."

The delay had been *just* enough though. Before Nip could fire, Gordon ducked and—as part of the same motion—lunged for the light switch. As the bullet soared over his head, he hit the switch, plunging the room back into a darkness as startling as the light had been.

Nip continued to fire, but Gordon stayed low. Although he couldn't see his attacker, he charged toward where Nip had been standing. He was able to tackle the monster and they wrestled on the ground, Gordon dislodging the hat.

"Hey, easy, I got that on the road down south," Nip said.

The hell is he talking about?

Nip was strong as hell, and he had the upper hand. After a brief scuffle Gordon was pinned and, although he couldn't see, he imagined he could feel the hot breath that meant Nip was about to bite off a chunk of his face.

Not going to happen.

Twisting his legs underneath, he shifted his center of gravity and managed to flip his opponent over. Nip's gun clanged to the floor, and following the sound, Gordon was able to grab it.

Then he was blinded.

The lights were on again.

"Drop it," a woman said.

Turning in the direction of the voice, Gordon squinted. Even before his eyes had adjusted, he could see that the woman was gorgeous. Tall, wavy blond hair, trim figure; she was dressed stylishly in a fitted blouse and skirt that went just below her knees.

She had four ears and canine teeth.

"I said drop it," the woman demanded. "I never miss the bullseye in target practice, so don't try me."

Gordon dropped the gun. Nip grabbed it and, shooting a malevolent glare over his shoulder, he went over to the woman.

"Way to go, Tuck."

"Nip and Tuck," Gordon said. "Cute."

"Cute?" Tuck said. "What the hell is *cute* about us?"

"Your names," Gordon said, and he got blank looks in return. "They were assigned to you by Hugo Strange."

Nip and Tuck exchanged looks, and started laughing.

Gordon remained deadpan. "Guess I don't get monster humor."

"We don't get *your* humor," Tuck said, composing herself.

"I wasn't trying to be funny," Gordon replied.

"Hugo Strange didn't give us our names," she said. "We know exactly who we are. Do you know who *you* are?" she added mockingly.

"Hate to burst your bubble, folks, but you've been brainwashed," Gordon said. "Sure, you *think* you're Nip and Tuck, but believe me, you're not. You're whoever the hell you were before Strange abducted you and messed with your heads, programmed your memories and created your personalities."

Nip and Tuck laughed again.

"Created our personalities," Nip said.

"I know," Tuck said, snorting. "Have you ever heard anything so ridiculous?"

"Maybe it sounds like bullshit," Gordon said, "but you have to believe me. I know first-hand, Strange screwed with my head too. The lunatic dosed me with truth serum, for God's sake. Who knows who you really are? Strange might know, but that sadistic loon isn't talking. You might have families—families who miss you and love you. If you do the right thing and turn yourselves in, there are doctors who can try to rehabilitate you."

They were listening. He had to keep going.

"You don't want to hurt more innocent people. Give yourselves up now, and I'll do everything I can to help."

He'd given the same spiel more times than he could count. None of the monsters had given themselves up—they were too far gone, trapped too deep in their delusions to be reached. After all, why should they feel the need to be cured, if they didn't think that there was anything wrong with them?

Gordon wasn't surprised when the two started laughing again.

"So *what*, then?" Tuck said. "You're saying we don't exist?"

"Yeah, I guess that means we're invisible," Nip said.

"Maybe we can walk through walls," Tuck offered.

"You say you want to help," she said to Gordon,

leaning in closer. "You just want to help yourself to the money. I'll tell you what I think, Mister Bounty Hunter—there's only one person in this room who's not going to exist real soon, and it's you."

"The real you isn't a killer," Gordon insisted. "Underneath somewhere there has to be a rational woman." But she wasn't buying it.

"Shut the hell up," she shouted. "It's time to stop messing around and get down to business." She turned to Nip. "Don't you think?"

"Yes indeed, baby."

They lifted their guns.

"Whoa, hold it now," Gordon said with his hand still raised. He had to buy time, or he was well and truly screwed. Not to mention dead. His only chance was if he could get to his gun, which lay on the floor a few feet away. Glancing up at the chandelier, he figured he only had one option.

"What is it now?" Tuck asked. "You wanna put us in touch with our feelings?"

"No, that ship has sailed," Gordon said, "but I do want to keep you from getting yourselves killed."

At that they gaped, and wavered just long enough to give Gordon his opening. He dove for his weapon, grabbing it as they opened fire. He rolled to his left. A barrage of shots rang out, but he managed to make it to cover behind a decrepit piano. Nip and Tuck continued to fire, not allowing him any opportunity to shoot back.

So instead he aimed up, at the wires holding the

chandelier. He didn't have Nip's genetically enhanced skills, so he fired several times in quick succession. The chandelier shook violently. Suddenly it fell from the ceiling, and came crashing down.

The light went dim, though a couple of the sconces along the wall stayed on, and there was sudden silence. Gordon peeked over the piano and, sure enough, the heavy chandelier had fallen directly onto his targets, crushing them to death.

He was happy to be alive, but he never felt happy about killing monsters. The bounties might be for "dead or alive," yet every death was a tragedy. What he'd said was true—these two hadn't chosen this fate. Hugo Strange had chosen it for them. And so, indirectly, had Thomas Wayne.

SIX

Stumbling out of the building, Gordon took stock. He had cuts and bruises all over him, but he was okay. More to the point, he was still breathing. Sirens sounded in the distance, coming closer. Maybe Bullock had sent him some backup.

Great timing.

He managed to make it to his car. Getting in, he pulled out his cell and hit a pre-programmed number.

"Harvey?"

"Jim, buddy, where the hell are you?"

"In my car."

"You mean *my* car."

It was true. Gordon had, well, *borrowed* Bullock's car when he headed south to meet Lee—to begin the rest of their lives together, he'd thought.

"Yeah, well," he replied, "I'll give it back to you, don't worry."

"I had to buy a new ride."

"Then I'll buy it from you."

"Yeah, you and all your bounty money," Bullock said. "You must be rolling in it with all those monsters you've been grabbing."

"Speaking of which, you busy, Harv?"

"What the hell do you think? The street's crawling with monsters, and only some of 'em are Strange's creeps. And *you* left me stuck with the—"

"In that case I have some good news for you," Gordon said, eager to head off his friend's tirade. "I just took two more off the grid."

"Must be something wrong with my connection," Bullock said, letting his breath whistle out. "It sounded like you said you took down *two* monsters, all by your lonesome."

"I did," Gordon replied. "You'll find them in a building by the docks, near Quincy. It's an old building, the one with a lamppost leaning against it. You can't miss it."

"How do you keep catching these bastards?" Bullock demanded. "Our guys haven't caught that many more than you have, and we've got the whole department working on it, night and day."

"What can I say? I guess I've finally found my calling," Gordon offered. "I thought I was meant to be a cop, but it looks like I was born to hunt monsters. Who'da thunk it? Oh, and one of them is the most wanted monster in Gotham."

"Hold your enchiladas," Bullock said. "You took down Nip? We've been trying to find that four-eared mass murderer for months now."

"Yeah, and get this," Gordon said, allowing himself

to grin. "Nip's girlfriend... Her name's Tuck."

"Of course it is," Bullock said. "It makes sense though. Nip's been spotted with a female accomplice, but we hadn't been able to ID her."

"Well, you can ID her now, after you dig her out from under the chandelier that crushed them to death."

"How the hell do you do it, Jim?"

"Not trying to make you look bad, Harv, I swear."

"If that's true, you're failing miserably."

"I'll make it up to you, big guy, I promise."

"There's an easy way to do it too," Bullock said.

Here it comes...

"Harvey, don't..."

"What can I say to get you back at your desk where you belong?" Bullock asked. "Gotham needs you, Jim, and working alone here, I feel like I'm just old raggy clothes pinned to a laundry line—you know, hung out to dry."

Gordon laughed. "Appreciate the sentiment, Harv, but Jim Gordon the cop is in the past. I have to focus on my dreams, not my memories."

"Where'd you get that from? A self-help book, or a bathroom wall?"

"My father actually."

"Oh," Bullock said. "Sorry, Jim. I was just busting your chops."

"Me too," Gordon said. "Actually I got it from a bathroom wall."

Bullock snorted out a laugh. "Son of a bitch, you got me."

When he let himself admit it, Gordon missed Bullock. The camaraderie, of course, but also the simple feeling of having a partner. Working with Bullock, it was sort of the feeling he got when he was in a great relationship—like with Lee. He felt like they were in synch, like they *got* each other. And they always had each other's backs.

He was spinning again, had to catch himself— ruminating about Lee had turned into an obsession, but he wasn't far enough gone not to realize that he had a problem.

"Seriously," Gordon said. "Just six months ago I was in a cell at Blackgate, serving a life sentence. That's not exactly the kind of guy you want working for the department."

"I get it that you don't want to go back to Blackgate, Jim," Bullock said, "but I know what kind of guy you are. You're *exactly* the kind of guy we want in the department. Hell, you're the kind of guy we *need* in the department."

"If I had any tears left in me, I'd be crying at that," Gordon responded. "Listen, right now I need to be on my own, and I need to hunt down some more monsters. Oh, and for the record, if anyone gives a damn, the kills tonight were in self-defense."

"Of course they were," Bullock said.

Gordon heard something in the background. "Where are you?"

"The street," Bullock said. "I'm, ah… about to head into Barbara Kean's new place."

Gordon tensed at the name of his psychotic ex, and his jaw went tight. He'd heard that Barbara and her girlfriend, Tabitha—Theo Galavan's unhinged sister—had opened a new club, but he hadn't been by out of sheer self-preservation.

"Good for her," he said, and he thought he might mean it. "Guess I'm not the only one in Gotham trying to reinvent myself."

"Yeah, well, we'll see," Bullock said. "Listen, Jim, we gotta catch up soon."

"You pick the spot, I'm there," Gordon said. "In the meantime, send some people over to clean up this mess by the docks. Make sure I get credit for the busts."

"You got it, Jimmy."

Gordon ended the call and shut off his phone. Now that the adrenaline rush had passed, his body ached like hell, but he'd be okay. He wetted a rag and wiped off as much blood as he could, and then turned the key, released the emergency brake, and drove away. He was hungry and one of his favorite greasy spoons— Donny's—was only a few blocks away.

Gordon had been to Donny's Diner dozens of times, usually with Harvey. The grub was cheap, but it didn't exactly cater to the elite of Gotham. It was the kind of place where you had to keep your head up at all times, and if you had any enemies, sitting facing the door was a pretty good idea.

When Gordon entered three guys spotted him and

immediately bolted out the back exit. This used to happen all the time when he was a GCPD detective, and a lot of people in Gotham still thought Gordon was a cop. The guys who'd bolted probably had warrants out for their arrest, but this wasn't his concern anymore. If they didn't have prices on their heads, he didn't give a damn.

He sat at the counter and Mike, the server, came over. They'd known each other for years. The man made the best damn cheeseburgers in Gotham.

"Hey, Jim, you okay?" Mike looked concerned. Gordon figured he probably still had blood on him.

"Oh, I'm fine," Gordon sad. "Nothing a Donny's double cheeseburger with double fries couldn't fix."

"You got it." Mike shouted the order to the cook, then turned back to Gordon. "Crazy times, huh?"

"Yeah," Gordon agreed, flashing back to Nip's bloody corpse. "Crazy's a good word to describe it."

"I haven't let my daughters out of the house since it all started," Mike said. "This city was dangerous enough before the monsters broke out, but now it's damned insane. I don't care how much school they miss. I'd rather have stupid kids than dead kids."

At that he went to clean the tables of the guys who'd taken off. Gordon took a look around the place. The usual Ls—lowlifes, loners, and losers—were huddled over their meals, all oozing misery. Then he turned to the left, noticing for the first time the only woman in the place. He didn't know how he'd missed her— maybe she'd gone to the bathroom and come back. She had wavy brown hair tied back in a ponytail and was wearing a conservative navy dress, as if she'd come here straight from work. She had a full cup of coffee in front of her and seemed agitated—fidgeting a lot and checking her watch.

It was unusual for a woman, especially an attractive woman, to be alone in a place like this, in this part of Gotham. While Gordon wasn't looking for anything romantic—the loss of Lee was too fresh in his mind for him to even consider it—he'd been spending a lot of time alone lately, and was in the mood for some company. So he went over to where the woman was sitting and showed his warm, dimpled smile that women always seemed to like.

"This seat taken?"

The woman glared in an almost hateful way. That surprised him. Sure, it could be taken as a cheesy pick-up line, but offensive?

"I'm sorry," Gordon said. "Did I—"

"No, it's okay," she replied, and her expression softened. "You just caught me off-guard." She still looked wary though.

"In this place it's a good idea to err on the side of caution," he said, "but I assure you I'm one of the good guys." Then he noticed her glancing at his sleeve. He looked down. There was a bloodstain, plain as day.

"That's just uh, um, ketchup." He smiled "So do you come here often?"

Now *that* sounded like a cheesy pickup line. He winced inwardly.

"No," she said. "I was just passing by and I was hungry so I came in here to get something to eat."

"Well, I'm sorry if I'm bothering you," he said. "I could just go back—"

"No, it's okay." She seemed a little sad.

"Rough day?"

"Why do you say that?"

"Just a vibe I'm getting."

She hesitated, then said, "Please join me."

"I'm Jim," he said, sitting next to her and holding out his hand.

"Clarissa." She accepted the handshake.

"Nice to meet you."

"Likewise."

"So my hunch was right, wasn't it?" Gordon said.

"About what?"

"You look like you've had a rough one."

"Look who's talking." Her gaze returned to the sleeve.

"Got me there," he confessed.

This time Clarissa didn't respond, not even with a little chuckle, which was what he'd hoped to get. She stared at the rows of drinking glasses glistening in the lights behind the bar. She seemed preoccupied again.

"You sure you're okay?"

"Yeah, yeah, I'm fine," Clarissa said, not sounding fine at all. "So do you work around here?"

"I guess you could say that… yeah, occasionally," Gordon said.

"What kind of work do you do?"

I'm a cop, Gordon thought. That answer almost seemed instinctual. It had been how he'd defined himself for years. It didn't seem as if *bounty hunter* would go over well, either.

"I'm a freelancer," he said.

"A freelancer? A freelancer doing what?"

"I mean, a collector," he said. "I collect money for my services." As the words came out of his mouth, he realized he wasn't doing himself any favors. She appeared confused, and understandably so.

"How about you?" he said, trying to steer the conversation in a different direction. "Actually, you look familiar."

"I do?"

"Yeah. So what kind of work do *you* do?"

She seemed uncomfortable with the question.

"What difference does it make?" she asked, looking at her coffee.

"Well, it doesn't make any difference at all," Gordon said, "except you asked me what I do, so I thought it was fair... Hey, it's okay if you don't want to—" Then it hit him. "Wait, I know where I've seen you—at Gotham Federal. You work there, don't you?"

"Yes," she said. "Yes, I do."

"You're a manager, right?"

"That's right."

"Okay, now it's all coming together," he said. "I... used to do my banking there. Wait, there was a robbery there today, wasn't there?" Abruptly Clarissa swiveled on the stool and looked away.

"Yes, there was a robbery," she said. "It was, well, it was extremely traumatic."

"I'm sure it was."

Clarissa turned back, and her eyes narrowed.

"Was that supposed to be a joke?"

"No," he replied quickly, "I'm sure it was stressful." He hoped he sounded sincere.

"And how would you be sure?" she said, her words coming out sharply. "Have you ever been in the middle of a shootout?"

Jim had to stifle a laugh. "Yeah," he said, "actually I have. Just a few times." The sarcasm went way over her head, and for that he was grateful.

"I thought I was going to die," she continued. "There were men with guns, and there were monsters. There was so much blood. I can't even count how many people died. It's a miracle I'm here right now."

Mike brought over Gordon's burger and fries.

"Thanks, buddy," Gordon said.

"For one of Gotham's finest, anytime," Mike said, then he walked away. She pinned Gordon with her gaze, all of the suspicion back, and more.

"You're a cop?" She didn't sound happy. Maybe even a little afraid.

"*Was* a cop," he answered. "So can you tell me about the monsters?"

Clarissa got up.

"What's wrong? What did I say?"

"It was nice meeting you," she answered, "but I have to go now."

"Why do you have to—"

"Goodbye."

She left a twenty on the counter and rushed out of the diner. As she did, Mike came over.

"Somebody's in a hurry," he said. "What'd you say to her, to chase her off like that?"

"I don't think it was something I said," Gordon responded. "I have a feeling it was the word 'cop' that scared her off, and not my personal charms."

"Hey, don't judge." Mike snatched the twenty. "All she had was coffee. The lady knows how to tip."

SEVEN

The monster's mouth was so close that Selina could smell its disgusting breath.

"Ugh," Selina said. "Ever think of using some mouthwash, dude?"

The monster wasn't a talker, but it backed up a little. Maybe it was just surprised because she didn't seem afraid of dying.

Without hesitating, Selina reached out and placed her hands on top of the thing's slimy bald head. Then she propelled herself up and over the monster and landed on her feet. Leaping up toward the fire escape, she grabbed the bottom rung. As she hoisted herself up, the monster grabbed her legs and hissed again. Selina tried to maintain her grip, but the bastard was strong, and she couldn't hold for much longer. She had to do something, and quick—

Bang! Bang!

As soon as the gunshots rang out, the monster let go of her and crumpled onto the pavement. Selina pulled herself up to the fire escape and looked down. It was Jimmy, the street kid from the pool hall. He was standing there, holding a gun.

"Thanks, man," Selina said. Then she thought about it and asked, "Why do you care?"

"I shouldn't," he said. "I shoulda just let that monster eat you up and spit you out, after what you did to me, disrespecting me in front of my friends."

"Ha," Selina said. "Who disrespected who? I only gave you what you deserved. Besides, you didn't have to do that. I had the situation under control."

Johnny laughed.

"What's so funny?"

"Come on, you're not serious, are you?" Johnny said. "That monster was about to kill you. There was nothing you could do about it."

"Yeah, well maybe that's how it looked," Selina said, "but appearances can be deceiving." Time to change the subject. "What're you doing here anyway? Were you following me?"

"What if I was?"

"What're you? Some kind of stalker?"

"That what you want me to be?" He grinned.

"Oh puh-leeze," Selina said. "Is that the best you got?"

"Okay, you wanna know the truth?" Johnny said. "I was following you 'cause I was mad at you and wanted to get back at you." He looked at the crumpled figure and scratched his head. "Doesn't seem like such a big deal now." Looking up again, he added, "Why don't you come down here so we can talk?" He walked over so that he was between her and the monster.

"Gee, so romantic," Selina said. "How can I resist?" Then her eyes went wide.

Behind Johnny, the monster stirred and started to get up, with blood or something oozing from its mouth. It crouched and tensed.

"Behind you!"

Johnny turned and shot the monster in the head at point-blank range. Brains and bone splattered as the thing jerked back. It wouldn't be getting up again.

Johnny looked at her. His eyes were wide and he was as white as a sheet. Selina knew how he felt, but she wasn't about to let him know that.

"Guess you should thank *me* now," she said. "I just saved your life."

"Man, these things are so disgusting," Johnny said. She waited for him to say more, but he remained silent, looking down at the corpse and shaking so much she was concerned the gun might go off again.

"Well, that's that," Selina said, and she turned to climb to the top of the fire escape. "See you never, Johnny."

"Wait, where you going?"

She stopped. "I got business to take care of."

"What kind of business?"

"Business business," Selina said. "But it's none of *your* business."

"Maybe I can go with you?" he suggested. "You never know when another monster's gonna jump out and attack you. I could help."

"Thanks, but no thanks," she replied. "I feel safer on my own."

"Hey, don't you wanna split the bounty with me?" he asked. "See what a nice guy I am? That's serious money, and even though you humiliated me in front of my friends, I'm willing to split it with you."

"You've got to be kidding," Selina said.

"What do you mean?"

"Think about it, dude," Selina said. "I know you don't have all the seeds in your apple, but a smart-ass guy like you, walking around with a gun. Is it legal? You got a rap sheet. About the minute you call 'em, the cops'll look you up. You probably did a stint already in juvie, maybe a couple stints. Am I right?"

"Yeah," Johnny said. "So?"

"So there's a couple of other bodies, along with the monster. Did you seem them? Cops'll accuse you of killing them, and even if they don't, do you think they'll really give you the bounty money? The whole thing's a big fix. People like us don't wind up with bounties. Those go to people like Jim Gordon."

Johnny looked confused, like he was struggling to understand what it was she was saying. He really wasn't the brightest bulb on the tree.

"Maybe you're right."

"There's no 'maybe' about it," Selina said. "I know I'm right." She turned again and scrambled up the fire escape with ease.

"Hey, when I can see you again?"

Selina didn't bother answering.

Even though Johnny was kind of cute, in a dumb brunette kind of way, the truth she'd never admit to anyone, ever, was that she missed Bruce Wayne. Maybe it was because Bruce, unlike any other boy she'd ever met, always surprised her. Most people were *what you see is what you get*, but not Bruce. He was like an onion. He had lots of layers and Selina enjoyed peeling them off one by one, trying to reveal the real Bruce Wayne buried deep inside.

Selina reached the top and vaulted over the edge, then sprinted across the wide expanse. She leapt from rooftop to rooftop till she got to the end of the block, then she descended a fire escape, and strolled out of another alley, walking casually along the street.

There was still a little time before she had to be at the meeting spot to split the loot from the robbery. She was hungry, so she stopped at a pizza place and had a couple of slices. At least eleven dollars was still enough for that.

"Selina Kyle."

She was leaving the pizza joint when she heard a man's voice. He sounded official—probably a cop. Nonchalantly, Selina turned and saw *two* GCPD officers, a thin guy and a heavyset woman. He was standing alongside a squad car, and she was just getting out of the driver's side.

Without missing a beat, Selina said, "No idea who that is, sorry," and she resumed walking.

"Hey," the woman said.

Selina turned again and said, "Look, I'm in kind of a hurry, lady."

"Don't 'lady' me. Do you have some ID?"

"Why would I have ID?" Selina said. "I don't drive yet, and I don't go to school." She hoped that would be the end of it, but no...

"You have a choice," the guy said. "You tell us your name, or we take you down to the station."

That didn't leave her any choice. If Selina didn't get to the meeting spot, she'd be out five hundred bucks. The quickest way out of this would be to just play ball.

"Yeah, I'm Selina Kyle, so what?"

The man pulled a walkie-talkie off of his belt. "Hey, we got the girl..." he said, then he put a finger to his earpiece. "Okay... Yeah. You got it."

"Who's he talking to?" Selina asked the woman.

"You're going to come with us," the woman said.

"Why?" Selina said. "I told you who I am."

"We're not going to the station," the man said.

"Then where we going?"

"You'll see when we get there," the woman replied. "Get in the car."

Selina thought about running, but decided it wasn't a good idea. If they caught her, she was toast. This way, at least, it might be quick. So she got in the back, and the cops got into the front, the female cop driving.

Selina didn't know if this had to do with the dead monster, the pool hall pickpocketing, or the bank robbery. She'd had a busy day and, until now, it had been a productive one, too.

"This better not take long," Selina said, "because I, like, have an appointment." The cops ignored her. They were headed toward the South Side, where she was supposed to meet her contact. Because of monster mania, the streets were emptier than usual, and they zipped along with siren on, going through red lights.

Within about ten minutes, the squad car double-parked on a side street in front of a playground.

"Why are we here?" she asked.

Again, the cops didn't answer, but they got out of the car. The female cop opened the door next to Selina.

"Get out."

As she did, she saw Harvey Bullock approaching her. He was easy to spot in his fedora and trench coat, and his scraggly beard looked scragglier than usual. Alongside him there was a dorky-looking guy with short blond hair. Selina had never seen him before.

"Thanks, guys, good work," Bullock said to the cops. "I'll take it from here." They got back into the squad car and drove away.

"Long time no see," Selina said. "I never got a chance to congratulate you on your big promotion."

"I haven't been missing sleep over it."

"You're the big captain now, right?" Selina laughed, then covered her mouth. "Sorry, I'm not trying to be rude or anything. It's just that 'captain' and 'Bullock' don't really go together."

The look on his face told her she was getting under

his skin, which was exactly what she intended to do. She liked the feeling of control.

"Guess your application got rejected," Bullock said.

"My application?"

"To charm school," Bullock said with a smirk.

She had to admit, it wasn't the worst comeback. Not the best, either, but for Bullock, it was like Shakespeare.

"Who's your new sidekick anyway?" She nodded toward the blond guy.

"I'm Officer Collins."

"Say hi to him now while he's above ground," Bullock said.

"I don't get it," Selina replied.

"Inside joke."

"Still not funny," Selina said. "It's just weird seeing you without Jim Gordon. I hear he's catching a lot more monsters than you. That must be tough on your ego, huh?"

"Cute as a freakin' button, aren't you?" Bullock said. "So who you hanging around with these days? I mean, besides Fish Mooney."

"What makes you think I'm back with Fish?"

"She's back on the grid, moving her way back up," he said. "Figured you'd want in on the action."

"Even if I was working with her, why's it your business?"

"If you were smart you'd stay far away from her," Bullock said. "Trust me, I know better than anybody how seductive Fish Mooney can be. But that's *exactly* why you gotta stay away from her. Fish like her, they're the ones you gotta throw back into the pond, the ones who mess with your head. Especially when they come back to life. I hear rumors she's *really* messing with people's heads," he added, "doing some serious mind control. Don't know if it's true, but after a stint with a weirdo like Hugo Strange, there's no telling what's possible."

"Sorry, Harvey, but I don't believe in that 'mind control' voodoo," Selina said, "and I haven't seen Fish in, like, forever."

"She's lying," Collins said. Bullock shot him an annoyed look, as if saying *shut up*.

"How do you know?"

"Used to play poker professionally," Collins said. "I'm good at tells. Her tell is her bottom lip. When she's not moving it, she's lying."

"'Course you did," Bullock said, and for some reason he looked annoyed. He turned back to Selina. "Okay, now it's time for you to be straight with us, tells or no tells," he said. "Who've you been hanging around with these days?"

"Why do you ask?" she countered. "You writing a book about me? If so, I want a cut."

"If I wrote a book, it sure as hell wouldn't be about you."

"What would it be about?"

"Maybe when you grow up, kid, I'll write it and you'll read it. Until then, you're too young."

"If you're as good at writing as you are at being a police captain, I'm sure it's gonna be a blockbuster," Selina said.

"Look, let's cut to the chase. I know you were a part of the crew that robbed Gotham Federal today. An officer and a bunch of civilians were killed, so right now you're an accessory to murder."

She kept her expression calm—especially her lower lip.

"I wasn't there."

"Lying," Collins said.

"Not."

"Okay, cool it, both of you," Bullock said. Then to Selina, "We know you were there—we've got eyewitnesses. Tell us what you know, or we'll have to take you in." Something in his voice made her think he regretted it a little.

"If you had any evidence against me, you would've taken me in already, instead of talking to me on the street. So let's just be real, all right?"

He frowned at her, then nodded. "We got eyewitnesses who said you caused a distraction at the bank, right before the robbery took place."

"Just a coincidence," Selina said.

"Lying again," Collins said.

She shot him a nasty look. Bullock glared at his pre-pubescent partner.

"You expect me to believe that you just *happened* to be outside Gotham Federal," Bullock said to her. "Then went inside at the exact same time a robbery takes place?"

"Maybe I was on my way there," Selina said.

"Yeah? You got an account there?"

"Maybe I was bringing in some rolls of quarters, and my buddy got hurt, just like I told the guard. Not my fault shit happened."

"Look, I know telling the truth isn't exactly your forte," Bullock said, "but we're gonna get the guys who did this, and if I find out you're lying—that you were in on that robbery—I'm not cutting you any deals. You're gonna go away till you're an adult, or *past* your adultery."

"My adultery? I'm not gonna be a cheater when I grow up."

"But you're still gonna be a liar. Same difference."

"Is that all you got?"

"No," Bullock said. "There's a lot more where that came from. If I find out you're keeping something from me about that robbery, I'm gonna throw the book at you."

"The book you're gonna write?"

"Lemme give you a little advice," Bullock said. "This whole routine you got going on, it might work for you while you're a teenager, but when you grow up it's gonna lose its charm. I know you don't have any parental figures, but there are people out there. I'm not talking about Arkham, but you might wind up there too, like your friend Barbara."

"I don't have friends," Selina said, "but thanks for the advice. I have an idea too. Maybe if this whole 'Captain Bullock' thing doesn't work out, you can start a second career as a life coach."

Collins snickered, and Bullock shut him up with a look.

"So if we're done, I've got places to be." She turned, and they didn't try to stop her, so she strutted away, acting like everything Bullock had said had bounced off her.

The truth was, the stuff about how she didn't have any parents stung... a little. Selina didn't mind being on her own. She'd been taking care of herself just fine, and she didn't need anybody around to be happy. As far as she was concerned, that was something to feel proud of.

Besides, it wasn't like kids with nice parents always ended up happy. Look at Bruce. Still, Selina didn't like to be reminded that she was an orphan. It brought back thoughts of her mother, and she was a lot happier going through life not thinking about that selfish bitch at all.

She ducked down another alley and climbed up a fire escape. She zigzagged across the rooftops, up and down a couple more fire escapes, just to make sure Bullock didn't have someone tailing her.

When she was certain she was in the clear, she headed to the meeting spot to get the rest of her cut.

EIGHT

Three days earlier…

Sometimes it seemed like every decision she made turned out to be a bad one. Case in point: her decision to date Eddie Logan.

Of course, Clarissa hadn't known Eddie was psycho when she met him. If he'd walked up at the New Year's Eve party and said, *"Hey, I'm Eddie, and I'm psychotic—what's your name?"* that would've been the end of it.

Instead he'd said, "Hey, I'm Eddie, how come we've never met yet?" In retrospect she wasn't sure why that worked any better. Sure, she'd been going through a rough time in her life. Her mother had just passed away, and her father was battling stage-four cancer. Her most recent boyfriend had left her for another woman, so she was at a particularly low point.

In retrospect, she might as well have had a bright-red target painted on her forehead.

Clarissa's father died, leaving her sad and alone,

and Eddie took advantage of it. Things had moved quickly—much *too* quickly—and after a couple of months they were living with each other. When her gut should've been telling her to slow down, she got caught up in the romance and, yes, the sex.

During a romantic trip upstate he proposed to her, and they began to plan their wedding. Around that time, she began to catch him in lies. Details about his past didn't add up, and he told her different versions of the same stories. The biggest lie revolved around his income. He told her he was a successful "investor," but it turned out he was beyond broke. He owed money to loan sharks.

More than a hundred thousand dollars.

She was angry, felt betrayed, but she couldn't leave him. Clarissa knew she was repeating her same old patterns, but she loved him and thought she could fix him. So she took money out of her retirement account to help him pay off his debts, but it wasn't enough. He was still over fifty thousand in debt.

Then one night, about a week ago, four men broke into their apartment. Two guys attacked Eddie, beating him mercilessly, while two guys held Clarissa, forcing her to watch. When they were done they said that if he didn't pay the rest by the end of the month, they'd kill him, rape her, and then kill her too. When the men left Clarissa wanted to call the police, but Eddie wouldn't let her.

"What're we going to do?"

"I have an idea," he said.

"What is it?" She was afraid to hear the answer.

Eddie's ideas never led to anything good.

"I know some guys."

It still didn't sound good.

"What guys?"

"Friends of friends, from The Bottoms." The Bottoms was a seedy bar where Eddie hung out a lot.

"I don't like the sound of any of this," Clarissa said.

"You'll see," Eddie said. "It'll solve all our problems, baby. I promise."

The next day Eddie took her for a drive to the outskirts of Gotham, an area where there were big industrial factories and not much else. He still wouldn't tell her where they were going, or why they were going there. They pulled into a big parking lot where one other vehicle—a van—was waiting. Eddie stopped some distance away and killed the ignition. Four men got out of the van and approached them.

"What's going on, Eddie?" Suddenly it felt like what had happened at the apartment.

"You'll see."

"What does that mean?"

He didn't answer. The group stopped about halfway between the two vehicles. They weren't the men from the apartment. There was a dark-haired, scruffy guy in jeans and a black leather jacket and a taller, older guy with thin gray hair. The other two were—

No, it can't be.

Although the group was only about twenty yards away, Clarissa squinted, making sure her eyes weren't lying.

"My God," she said. "Are they… are they *monsters*?"

"Don't worry about it."

There was no doubt about it. One was green—like the color of broccoli. The other looked animal-like, with a snout and other features of a dog or wolf.

"Are you *crazy*?" Clarissa hissed, afraid to raise her voice even though the men were too far away to hear. "If you see a monster, you're supposed to run the other way and call the police. These things are psychotic, they'll kill us."

"It's not like that," Eddie said. "I met them the other day. Not the sharpest tools in the shed, but they got them trained."

"Who's *they*?"

"Just trust me, all right?"

"One thing I'll never do is trust you," Clarissa said.

"Talkin' about us?"

She jumped and almost screamed. While she and Eddie had been arguing, the four had walked the rest of the way to the car. It was the scruffy, younger guy who spoke. He looked smug, arrogant. Clarissa already hated him.

Eddie opened the door and climbed out of the car. She noticed he left the keys in the ignition, causing the alarm to *ping*. Reluctantly Clarissa followed suit, walking around the back—away from the newcomers—to stand beside him.

"This your wife?" Scruffy Guy asked.

"Fiancée," Eddie said.

"*Ex*-fiancée," Clarissa said.

"Ouch," Scruffy Guy said.

He and the older guy laughed, but the monsters remained silent. Could they even understand English? From what Clarissa had heard, some of the monsters couldn't speak, but others had exceptional verbal skills and could even be considered geniuses. She was trying to avoid making eye contact with them, fearing it might incite them to… what? But like a car accident, she couldn't stop looking.

"This is Nick," Eddie said.

"Pleasure," Scruffy Guy said to Clarissa, smiling in a smarmy way.

"And this is Philip," Eddie said.

"Filippo," the older guy said.

"Sorry," Eddie said.

"Who the hell are these guys?" Clarissa demanded. "Why did you bring me here?"

"Looks like there's trouble in paradise," Filippo said. His voice sounded coarse, probably from smoking. His teeth were stained yellow.

Nick seemed confused. "You didn't tell her?"

"I figured we might as well, um, fill her in when we got here," Eddie said.

"Fill me in on what?" Clarissa said. "What the *hell* is going on here?"

"This ain't cool," Nick said to Eddie. "I just wanna do a job. I'm not here to be your goddamn marriage counselor."

"Job?" Clarissa looked at Eddie, but he avoided her gaze. "What kind of job?"

"Tell her, will ya?" Nick said. "Or the deal's off, and

I'll let these monsters decide what to do with you."

Clarissa couldn't resist glancing at the creatures, and it seemed to her that they suddenly looked ravenous. The doglike one was actually drooling.

She thought she might throw up.

"It's a bank job," Eddie said. "These guys are gonna rob Gotham Federal two days from now and you're gonna help them. Our share of the take'll get us out of debt."

"Us?" Clarissa glared at him. "*Us? Are you out of your mind?*"

"We've got no choice," Eddie said.

"You don't have a choice, but I do," Clarissa said. "Don't bother coming home later, the lock won't work."

Clarissa moved toward the car, or at least tried to. Eddie rushed up from behind and grabbed her.

"Baby," he said, "what're you doing?"

"Get your hands off me—and I'm certainly not your baby."

Eddie didn't let go.

Almost whispering, he said, "He's not kidding around, baby—I mean, sweetie. If you try to leave, those monsters'll kill both of us. I don't think you wanna die tonight, do ya?"

"I'm not robbing my bank," Clarissa said.

"You really want to take that chance?"

Clarissa glanced back. Now they were both drooling. She was sure of it.

"You got us into this," she said, "you get us out of

it. Tell them we're not interested."

"Hey," Nick called out. "What's goin' on over there? I got a date waiting for me at a hotel downtown, and she charges by the hour, whether I'm there or not."

"We'll be right there, don't worry. Just one second," Eddie yelled back.

"I'm not the one who should worry."

Eddie turned back to Clarissa. "I don't think you understand what's going on here," he hissed. "There's no such thing as 'not interested.' Once I said, we're in, we're in, there's no turning back."

"Why can't you just—"

"'Cause we know about it already, that's why. About them. They're not gonna let us walk out of here alive and take the chance that we'll rat them out to the cops. If we don't go along with it, the monsters are gonna kill us, and there won't be enough left to ID."

"You keep saying 'we,'" Clarissa said. "Are you robbing the bank too?"

"No," Eddie said. "I'm just supplying you."

"*Supplying* me?"

"Hey," Nick said, "I'm not sure I can control these guys much longer. You got twenty more seconds."

The monsters didn't move a muscle. Perhaps they didn't understand what Nick had said about them, or maybe they just didn't care. Either way, Clarissa was pretty sure she'd never get out of there alive.

"Come on, baby," Eddie said, pleading now. "We have to go along with it, and it's all going to work out, I promise. I've known these guys a long time. They know what they're doing. If I thought there was a chance of you getting hurt, you know I wouldn't let you get involved."

"Like hell you wouldn't."

She looked at him, at the car, at the monsters.

"But I'll do it."

Clarissa didn't see what choice she had. Right now she had to agree to the plan and make it convincing, just so she could get out of there alive.

"Thank you, baby," Eddie said. He tried to kiss her, but she pushed him away. He looked confused for a minute, then shrugged.

Imbecile.

Clarissa and Eddie returned to where the men and monsters were still waiting.

"Okay, she's in," Eddie said.

"Smart decision," Nick said. "Better off cooperating than dying, right?" Then he said to the monsters, "Sorry, boys, you'll have to wait a little longer for your next meal." The bigger one sneered, as if disappointed. He definitely seemed to understand what was going on.

"So what do you want me to do?" Clarissa asked.

"Your part is simple," Nick said. "All you've gotta do is let us into the vault area in the back. Everyone'll think we're forcing you, so no one will ever be the wiser.

"You gotta make it look legit though," he added. "It's gotta go quickly. GCPD response that time of day, we'll have at most six minutes to get in and out of the bank. That's why we need somebody on the inside, so there are no delays."

"What's my cut?" Clarissa asked.

Nick laughed. "The straight lady wants to know what her cut is?"

Filippo laughed too.

"You get twenty grand," Nick said.

"You told me fifty," Eddie said.

"Well, I changed my mind. What're you gonna do about it? Play ball, or become the next meal?"

"It's not fair," Clarissa said.

"Fair?" Nick said. "This ain't a wrestling match. You can't complain to the referee. This is whatcha call a dictatorship. It's gonna happen on Monday, and you'll do your part."

"That's our big day," she said, "before the Brinks truck arrives."

"I know it is," Nick said. "We've been watching for weeks. We know your routines, probably better than you do."

"I'm not doing it for a penny under fifty."

"*Baby*," Eddie pleaded.

"Shut up," Clarissa said. Then she said, "Fifty or no deal."

"That's an unfortunate decision." Nick raised his fist toward the monsters. "Okay boys... sic 'em."

The shorter monster lunged, grabbing Eddie by the throat.

"God, no," Eddie wailed. It quickly became an incoherent gurgle. The dog-man handed him to the gigantic, multi-colored monster, who lifted Eddie over his head and was about to throw him at a lamppost. Eddie was gasping, trying to scream.

Part of Clarissa wanted to let them tear Eddie to shreds. It was what he deserved for getting her into this mess. Yet despite everything, she still cared about the asshole, and she couldn't let him die.

"All right, tell them to stop," Clarissa said. "We'll take twenty, we'll take twenty."

"Heel," Nick commanded.

The big monster seemed disappointed, but he obeyed and lowered his captive to the ground, setting him on his feet. Eddie gasped, sucking in air, rubbing his neck. Unsteadily he returned to stand alongside Clarissa.

She didn't even look at him.

"You'll get a call in the morning, with further instructions," Nick said to her. "It's gonna be a real pleasure to work with you, I can tell already." Then he turned to the monsters and pointed. "Get into the van, *now*."

Like well-trained dogs they followed his orders.

"When do I get my money?" Clarissa asked.

"After the job, we're gonna meet at Dennis Drive, under the overpass, and divide all the... you know... *proceeds*."

"Divide with who?" Clarissa asked.

"You've got too many questions."

"I don't like to be in the dark."

"Then you're in the wrong city, sweetheart," Nick said.

"How do I know you'll show up?" Clarissa asked.

"You know who we are. What we look like. That's enough."

"How is that fair?"

"See, that's your main problem, lady," Nick said. "You think life's fair."

"What will stop you from killing me?"

"I could," Nick admitted, "but I don't want to go away for murder. I believe in forming relationships. If this works out, maybe we can do business again sometime. Maybe the next time you'll get a better deal. One that's more *fair*." He chuckled at his own joke. Then he turned and followed Filippo to join the monsters in the van. The engine rumbled to life, and they drove away.

Clarissa and Eddie watched them go then returned to their car. Without a word Eddie drove them out of the lot and back onto the highway. Up ahead, the Gotham skyline was bleak and smoggy. It looked as if the city was smoldering.

They didn't say anything for at least ten minutes.

"That was a stupid risk you took," Eddie said.

Clarissa did a double take. *Is he for real?*

"I took a stupid risk?" she said.

"Yeah," he said. "I mean, it was ballsy of you, but you gotta know when you have leverage in these situations and when you don't. When you don't have leverage, you can't afford to take risks. Damn near got me killed."

"You gambled money you didn't have, getting us into this mess, and I'm the one taking unnecessary risks?" She stared at the street ahead. "You're lucky I didn't just let you die."

Silence.

"Whatever," Eddie said after a while. "In the end, it'll all work out. Twenty ain't bad. It'll get the loan sharks off my back for a while, anyway, while we figure out a way to get the rest of the money."

"There you go again with the 'we.'" She frowned. "*We* is over, Eddie. From now on it's just *you*, alone, by yourself without me."

"Come on, baby, you don't mean that." He rested his right hand on her thigh. It felt like a clamp.

"Get your disgusting, filthy paw off me," she said.

He left it there for several seconds, just to be a jerk about it, then moved it back to the steering wheel.

She hoped he'd gotten the message.

It was dark by the time they got back to the apartment. Clarissa made Eddie sleep on the couch.

She wanted to go to the police, but she didn't know if this was a legitimate option. Would they really protect her? Maybe they would for a little while, but as soon as the protection ended, she and Eddie would probably wind up in a ditch.

There was no choice but to go along with the plan. She didn't kick Eddie out, either. Was it possible to love somebody and hate them at the same time? While she hated him for dragging her into all this, she still loved him. Perhaps the robbery would go smoothly, they'd pay off the loan shark, and get on with their lives. Maybe this was just one big, ugly bump in the road.

NINE

One Day Earlier…

The night before the robbery, Clarissa didn't sleep much, if at all. She couldn't really tell. She kept thinking about Nick's call, about the instructions he'd given her. She felt guilty and hated herself, and she hadn't even done anything yet. How would she feel tomorrow?

Finally, she gave in, got up, and got ready for work. When she was about done she went into the living room. Eddie was sprawled on the couch in his underwear, passed out. The whole apartment reeked of alcohol that had to be oozing out through his pores by now. This situation was so messed up, she thought darkly. She was about to risk her life because of a mess he'd created, and he planned to spend the morning on the couch, sleeping in.

Yeah, right.

Clarissa went into the kitchen and returned with two frying pans. Standing next to Eddie, she swung them wide, then clanged them together right over his head. The impact ran up through her arms, and she almost dropped one of them.

Eddie jumped and almost fell off the couch. Disoriented, he looked around frantically.

"Wha... What?" He grabbed his head as if in pain. "*What?*"

"Sorry to wake you," Clarissa said.

"Wha—what time is it?"

"Time for me to go to work."

"Work?"

Was he kidding?

"The bank? You remember what day today is, don't you?"

"Oh, right." He lay back and gingerly rubbed his temples. "Okay... Good."

"Good?" Clarissa said. "That's all you have to say? You should've woken *me* up today, with breakfast in bed. You should've given me a long massage or something, to show how much you appreciate me. You *owe* me, Eddie."

He sat up. "I do appreciate you, baby." He belched. "Oh, sorry 'bout that."

"You're disgusting."

She turned to walk away.

"Wait, come here," he said. "Gimme those." He took the frying pans from her and placed them on the couch. Then he held her hands and pulled her in close.

"I wish I'd never met you," she said.

"You don't mean that."

"I do mean it," she said.

"I appreciate you—really I do."

"I don't believe it."

"Well, maybe someday you will."

She didn't want to let him kiss her, but she didn't try to stop him either.

Arriving for work, Clarissa tried to act like it was just another day.

"Morning," she said to Harry, the guard.

"Morning, Clarissa," he said. Harry had been working at the bank long before Clarissa had started there. Next year he was planning to retire and move out west.

Inside, she said hello to Jack and Maria, two of the loan officers, and then she went into the secured area in the back. She said hi to a few tellers who were busy setting up for the day, then she poured herself her usual cup of coffee and sat at her desk.

Clarissa hated what she was about to put her colleagues through. She'd always considered herself to be a good person, with profound empathy. She wasn't deceitful and rarely lied. She prided herself on being trustworthy and reliable. She was kind to her friends and family, never littered, rarely cursed, and— until today—had never committed a crime, not even a speeding ticket.

Clarissa *still* hadn't committed a crime.

There was still time to get out of it. She could call the police right now, tell them the truth. When Nick and the rest of his crew arrived, they would be arrested on the spot. Almost certainly, this would put her life and Eddie's life in jeopardy, but wasn't it better to die and do the right thing, than to live and do the wrong thing?

She lifted the receiver and hit the buttons.

Nine…

One…

Then she hung up.

Clarissa was shaking and felt hot all over. Her hands were sweaty, and she could feel it dripping down the back of her neck.

Backing out now wasn't an option. She'd been debating this in her head for the past two days and always arrived at the same conclusion—it simply wasn't possible. Although she'd be throwing away everything she thought she was, she had no choice. She'd always put other people's needs first—that's what empaths did—but for once in her life it was time to put herself first. She'd been lonely for years, had endured a string of failed relationships since college. When she'd met Eddie she'd felt certain that she'd finally met "the one" and that her romantic losing streak was over.

She still loved him and wanted to have a future with him.

That would only be possible if they stayed *alive*. So she decided—for the umpteenth time—that she had to go through with the plan and pray for the best. Just like she was great at what she did, working as bank manager, she had to hope Nick was great at what he did. That the robbery would take place without a hitch. They'd get all the money from the safe, and then

Clarissa would claim her share, and that would be the end of it.

The police wouldn't suspect that Clarissa was involved—why would they?—and she and Eddie could live the rest of their lives in peace. He would pay off his bookie and get a good job somewhere and start to earn a respectable living. At his core Eddie was a great guy. He'd just made a few bad decisions.

After lunch Clarissa conducted a staff meeting, which was a nice distraction for a while. Then, at two o'clock she made sure no one was watching and slipped into the maintenance room. She knew exactly how to disable the Wayne Security system because it had been repaired just a few weeks ago. The repairmen had given her thorough instructions.

I wonder if Nick knows that. Maybe he was watching the whole time. The thought made her shiver. She disconnected several wires and then left the room and returned to the front of the bank.

Looking up, trying not to be obvious about it, she saw tiny red lights on the cameras. Glancing around the room, she suddenly felt panic begin to well up in her. She wasn't the only one who noticed. Roger, a loan officer, approached her, glancing up.

"Hey, Clarissa," he said, far too loudly. "I think the security system's on the blink."

She squinted as if confused. "What do you mean?" It sounded convincing, she thought. It was frightening how good she was at lying and deceit.

"The little red lights," Roger said. "Look."

Clarissa peered at one of the cameras. "Look at that; you're right." She made a point of checking another, then another. "And the system was just inspected a couple of weeks ago." She put on an exasperated expression. "See that's the problem with technology—machines always break. Thanks, Roger. I'll call our rep at Wayne Security."

It was 2:09 and the robbery was set to begin in fifteen minutes. The response time for Wayne Securities would be about an hour, so Clarissa felt confident that she could report the issue immediately, and thus allay suspicion. She made a display of calling in the work order, making sure a couple of people overheard her.

At exactly 2:23 a familiar van pulled up in front of the bank.

At 2:24, a teenage girl entered the bank. She was wearing a black leather jacket, a black turtleneck, and a black wool hat. She approached Harry.

"Help, my friend was just hit by a car!"

Clarissa didn't think she sounded convincing. Was this part of the plan? Nick hadn't mentioned anything about the involvement of a girl, but it seemed way too coincidental that she just happened to show up a minute before the robbery had been planned to begin. Under that tough, street kid exterior, the kid was attractive too. Clarissa wondered how she'd gotten mixed up with these scumbag bank robbers and their pet monsters.

Then again, Clarissa was mixed up with them too.

She hated that she knew so few details about the plan. A type-A person, she liked to feel in control. In this case, she was just an actress who had received only her own lines. All she knew was her part in the script, which made her feel very out of control—a feeling she didn't like.

Harry rushed outside. Through the window Clarissa watched two men exit the van, both wearing black ski masks. One of the men—it looked like Filippo—injected Harry with something. Harry collapsed, and they stuffed him in the van. The whole thing only took seconds.

Clarissa wanted to scream, but didn't. She had to stay in control, in character, or the whole plan would go bust.

Poor Harry! The man had worked hard for years and had never harmed anyone. All he wanted to do was retire and play golf, and now he might not even survive the day. If Nick had told her about this part of the plan, would she have gone through with it? Morosely she realized she probably would have. Staying alive was a powerful motivator.

The two guys in the masks entered the bank.

"This is a stick up," the short guy bellowed. Nick— he was carrying a duffel bag. "Everybody, face first on the floor!" A ripple of panic ran through the crowd. Someone screamed, then stifled it.

The customers and bank employees lay on the

floor. Even the girl—maybe she *wasn't* involved. Clarissa joined them and tried to appear appropriately panicked. This wasn't difficult because she was panicked. As Eddie would have said, *"Shit got real."*

Then the monsters came through the revolving door. A bunch of people shrieked, and Nick fired his gun at the ceiling a couple of times.

"The next guy who screams, gets one between the eyes!" he shouted angrily. In the ensuing silence Clarissa heard whimpering.

No, she thought. *No, no, nonono…*

It was a thin, elderly gentleman with a tweed jacket, glasses, and a gray beard. Nick heard the sounds, walked over, lifted his gun, and shot the old man between the eyes. The back of his head erupted in a spray of blood, brains, and skull fragments. Nick held his gun up again and scanned the stunned crowd.

"Anybody else wanna meet their maker today?"

There wasn't a sound.

"I didn't think so."

As Clarissa gaped, he stalked over to where she was lying. She flinched, and it didn't take any acting.

"You, get up."

She got to her feet as quickly as she could, afraid of what might happen if she didn't perform to his satisfaction. He shoved the bag into her hands.

"Empty all the drawers as fast as you can, and then the safe," he growled. Then he pointed his gun directly at her. "If you try to push an alarm, *everybody* gets shot."

"Yes, sir, right away."

Having something to do helped her calm down. Everything was going according to plan. No one would know that she was in on the robbery; how would they? She went behind the plexiglass into the tellers' area. There she did as she had been told and filled the bag with cash, focusing on larger bills.

"Police, drop your weapons."

Clarissa froze. That did *not* sound like part of the plan. She saw a young guy, a customer in the bank, standing up and displaying a badge. He looked every bit as scared as she felt. She knew all hell was about to break loose, but helplessly knew she couldn't do anything about it.

Regret overwhelmed her. Regret for not calling 911 when she'd had the chance. Regret for helping Eddie. Regret for saying yes to Eddie's marriage proposal.

"Police, drop your weapons!"

Nick and Filippo didn't drop their guns. Nick just peered over at the monsters and gestured with his head.

"Sic 'im," he said. The two creatures left their places by the door and began to circle the poor man.

"Stay back!"

The officer's gun pointed at one of his attackers, then the other, then back again. Finally panic got the better of him, and he started shooting. Most of his shots went wide, and the ones that struck home didn't have the desired effect. In fact, it was just the opposite.

Roaring like the monsters they were, the two started picking people up and throwing them around the room. Victims struck pillars and countertops with sickening thuds. People began screaming, scrambling for the door, forming a logjam. The young girl was nowhere to be seen, and Clarissa hoped she wasn't among the dead.

Nick and Filippo tried to shoot the cop, but hit innocent bystanders instead. The officer ran out of bullets, and the taller monster grabbed him by the arms, picking him up and hefting him over his head.

"No, please," the officer begged. "I'm sorry, I won't... I have a wife!"

The green monster flung him through the front window of the bank. The impact shattered the glass, and he landed with a sickening *thud* onto the sidewalk. That released the logjam, as people escaped through the shattered window. Not all of them made it though—Clarissa saw the doglike creature take a huge bite out of someone's face.

She turned away to avoid vomiting.

TEN

By the time the police arrived Nick, Filippo, and the monsters were long gone. Harry was nowhere to be seen, and she assumed they would find his body lying in a ditch, maybe even half-eaten.

Clarissa answered all of the questions they asked her, even mentioning the problem with the security system, since it already was a matter of record. She really was in a numb state of shock, so she didn't need to do any acting. She just had to cherry-pick the facts, making sure they all fell in the right order and added up properly.

Finally, they let her go, and she decided she wasn't ready to go home. So she drove to Donny's, an out-of-the-way diner. She liked it because it was in a dodgy part of town where nobody would recognize her. She hoped to sip a cup of coffee and mind her own business.

Her luck, she sat down next to a chatty guy named Jim, who happened to be a cop. She began to panic, then he explained that he was an *ex*-cop, but it was still way too close for comfort. Worse, he recognized her from Gotham Federal.

She left a big tip for the server and slipped away.

Leaving the diner, heading into the dimly lit parking lot, she felt as if she'd dodged a bullet. Even so, it didn't feel like her problems were fading away. It felt like she was getting in deeper and deeper.

"Clarissa."

The voice came from behind her, and it wasn't the guy named Jim. It was a male voice that sounded deep, tough, and menacing. Taking a deep breath, she turned slowly and saw two muscular scary-looking men. They both had bare arms and bald heads displaying what she thought must have been prison tattoos. One had a goatee. They were both ugly as hell. Their motorcycles were parked off to the side.

"Who are you?" she asked. "How do you know my name?" At least they didn't seem like cops, but she feared they had something to do with Nick and the robbery.

"Our names ain't important," the clean-shaven one said. He was the one who'd said her name.

"Where's the money at?" the one with the goatee demanded.

She decided to play dumb. What choice did she have?

"Money," she said. "What money?"

The guys opened big switchblades.

"Look, honey," the clean-shaven one said. "We don't got time for no games. He said you were picking up the money. That's why you went into the diner, right?"

"He?" Clarissa asked. "Who's he?"

"You know who," the guy with the goatee said. "Eddie."

Son of a bitch. Really? Eddie had told these guys about the robbery. After all she'd done for him, and all she'd done to save the relationship… *That bastard.*

Clarissa turned and sprinted toward her car.

She didn't make it. The goatee guy grabbed her from behind and put a cold blade against her neck.

"Honey, I don't think you understand the way this works."

"No, I don't think you guys understand." The voice was familiar. "Drop the weapons."

Jim, the ex-cop, stood just a few feet away. The bikers spun to face him, turning Clarissa with them, still with the blade held up to her neck.

"The hell are you?" the man with the goatee asked.

"I'm the guy with a gun. The guy who doesn't give a damn who gets hurt," Jim said. "Let the lady go."

"Wait, I know this guy," the clean-shaven one said. "He's Jim Gordon. He used to be a detective, then he went away to lockup for killing Mayor Galavan. Now he's a nobody." He grinned at that.

"Yeah, you're right," his partner said. "Hey, what're you waiting for? Get outta here, you washed up loser."

"Last time I'll ask politely," Gordon replied. "Let the lady go."

"We ain't lettin' nobody go," the clean-shaven one said. "And why're you callin' the shots anyway? How 'bout this one? How 'bout you drop your gun when I count to three or I'll gut this lady like a fish."

Gordon believed he'd do it, but he couldn't back down.

"One... two... Okay, you did this not me...." He put the tip of the blade against her throat, about to push it through. "Three."

He had no choice. An innocent life was on the line. Gordon fired twice in quick succession. The bullets hit them in the arms, causing them to squeal in agony and drop the blades. Non-lethal shots, but they'd hurt like hell. He lowered the gun.

"Y-y-you crazy, man?" goatee guy said.

"Quite possibly yes," Gordon responded. "Do you really want to test me?"

Gordon lifted his pistol again. The bikers exchanged looks of horror, then Clarissa's captor dropped her, letting her hit the pavement. The two made a mad dash to their bikes. They kicked them into life, and sped away.

"You all right?" Gordon asked.

"Fine," she replied, slowly coming to her feet, "but I had that under control." Knowing who he was now, she was warier than before.

"Funny, it didn't seem like you had it under control."

"You could've killed me."

"They could've killed you too," Gordon said. "Sometimes you have to choose your poison."

"Good point," she had to admit. "I guess I should thank you." She paused, then added, "Thank you. There, I said it."

"Appreciated," he said. "So what did they want from you?"

Clarissa hesitated, then said, "I—I don't know. Maybe they were just trying to rob me." She didn't know how much he'd heard.

"Why do I think you're lying?"

"Excuse me?"

"Look, if you're in trouble, I might be able to help."

"There's no need," she replied. "It was just a simple mugging. I should be going now." She walked over to her car, trying not to show how much she was shaking. Unlocking the driver's-side door, she opened it.

"Just be careful," Gordon said. "Something doesn't feel right. Whatever it is, you might not know what you're dealing with. Here, at least take my number. Call me if I can help." He held out a card.

"Thanks," Clarissa said, taking it, "but I can take care of myself just fine."

Driving away, Clarissa tried to make sense of what had just happened. Had Eddie really sent those thugs after her, to rob her and maybe kill her? Why would he do that, when they were on the same side, and the money was going to pay off his debts? It didn't make sense. There had to be more to it.

She drove fast at first, then slowed to within the speed limit and was careful not to run any red lights. The last thing she needed now was to get pulled over by a cop. She hoped Gordon wasn't too suspicious.

Even if he did suspect something, what could he do about it? He wasn't a police officer. He was just a citizen, like anyone else. He wasn't a threat.

She needed to stay positive. She had to believe everything would work out in the end, and that the run-in with the bikers didn't really mean anything. Yet she had an overwhelming feeling this was just the beginning of her nightmare.

That things were about to get much, much worse.

INTERLUDE

Since the murder of his parents, Bruce Wayne hadn't even considered returning to Switzerland, or anyplace else, for that matter. Back in Gotham, Bruce kept himself distracted with school and his passion for trying to track down the man who had killed his parents.

Here in Switzerland, however—perhaps *because* his mind wasn't preoccupied—the memories flooded back.

"I think I should sell the chalet," Bruce said to Alfred Pennyworth, his butler and legal guardian.

Alfred sat in an armchair, reading from a first edition of Joyce's *Ulysses*. He glanced over the top of his reading glasses, appearing startled. They were in the chalet's spacious drawing room. A fire was crackling in the fireplace and the snowfall outside had intensified. Combined with what they had received in previous storms, a few feet had accumulated.

"Sell it?" Alfred asked. "Why in god's name would you want to do that, mate? Why, just this morning on the slopes you remarked how beautiful it was in the Alps, how this is one of the most beautiful spots on earth."

"The beauty here is undeniable," Bruce said. "It's the memories that haunt me."

A few tears dripped down Bruce's cheeks.

Sometimes it seemed as if he hadn't had a chance to actually mourn the murder of his parents. Certainly he hadn't gone through the so-called "five stages" of grief. He'd cried that night in the alley, after the killer had shot Martha and Thomas Wayne in cold blood. During the months that followed, many nights he'd cried into his pillow as he fell asleep, but perhaps because he'd so preoccupied himself with trying to track down those responsible for his parents' murders, he had been stuck in the anger and denial stages.

Alfred placed the book, face open onto his lap.

"It's good to let it all out, Bruce," he said. "It's a *good* thing to feel your emotions. A lot of people can't."

"I'll be okay."

"I have no doubt you will. Regarding the chalet, you're bloody lucky you have good memories here. How many people have unhappy childhoods? You have parents who loved you, who only wanted the very best for you. You should cherish your memories instead of running away from them. Running away never solves anything now, does it?"

"Then why did we leave Gotham?" Bruce asked.

"Crikey, not with that again," Alfred said. "I go to all this trouble, making this poignant speech, and now you're going to rain on my parade, are you?"

"Part of the reason we left Gotham was to find

the connection between Hugo Strange and Wayne Enterprises," Bruce insisted. "The trail can't remain cold forever. If we'd stuck with that, we would've—"

"Gotten absolutely nowhere while you continued to fall behind on your studies."

"I could have focused in Gotham."

"With monsters running amok? I don't think so."

"Then my studies could've waited."

"Brilliant, and you'd fail out of school and there'd be *another* mess for me to resolve."

"You don't have to resolve my messes."

"Yes I do."

They fell silent as Bruce and Alfred just stared at each other. After a time, however, they relaxed, tension dropping visibly from their shoulders.

"Look, Alfred, I just don't belong here," Bruce said finally. "Maybe it has nothing to do with the memories after all. Maybe it has to do with what we left undone back in Gotham. We still don't know who was responsible for my parents' murder. The secret council wanted me dead, so it's possible they were the ones who hired—"

"The hit man who murdered your parents," Alfred said.

"So you agree with me," Bruce said.

"I agree that you have to let it go, at least for now," Alfred said. "You need to catch up on your studies, and I need to look after you. When we return to Gotham we can revisit the subject."

"I want to return immediately, Alfred."

"There are monsters running rampant in the city. It's bloody chaos."

"All the more reason I want to be there."

"I've already put you in enough danger since your parents died. It's time I do the job I promised them I'd do, and protect you properly."

"I'm not afraid of monsters."

"I don't doubt that."

"Then let's go back."

"We're not going anywhere."

"Why not?"

"Because I said so, that's why!"

Raising his voice, especially to Bruce, was out of character for Alfred. He put the book aside, went over to the bar, and poured himself a scotch on the rocks. He took a long sip as he gazed out at the snowstorm, then he turned back.

Bruce hadn't moved. He was still processing how he felt about the outburst, and what it meant.

"I'm sorry about that, Master Bruce," Alfred said. "I'll do a better job of controlling my temper the next time."

"It's okay, Alfred."

"I suppose the subject is a bit sensitive for me." Alfred finished the drink with a final gulp, then added, "Before your father was killed, I made a promise to him. It's a promise I take quite seriously and intend to keep. Thomas Wayne knew very well how dangerous Gotham was, and he knew it had the potential to become even more dangerous. He knew the incident with Karen Jennings was just the beginning. Even if he didn't know what was happening at Indian Hill, he knew bloody well that Hugo Strange was unstable and potentially dangerous."

Alfred continued. "By God, look how prescient he was. Strange's monsters running amok in the streets—robbing, assaulting, even *killing* innocent people. Even before that happened, he was worried about you growing up in this dark, corrupt world and was concerned that, as the wealthiest citizen of Gotham, you'd become a primary target. Lo and behold, he was right about that too. You were almost murdered by Galavan, that lunatic Jerome, and then Edward Nygma nearly gassed you and Lucius Fox to death at Arkham. You could've been killed in a nuclear explosion if Hugo Strange had gotten his way.

"On several other occasions during the past year, you've narrowly escaped with your life. I promised your father I'd look after you and, given all the evidence, I don't think I've done a very good job of it, have I? It was time to take the safe option for a change, Master Bruce. Not just for you. We both needed to find a place where we could recharge our batteries."

Bruce shook his head. "Nevertheless, it just feels wrong. Gotham's my home, and it's under siege. I should be there to help defend it."

"Defend it?" Alfred said. "You're bloody sixteen years old."

"That's irrelevant," Bruce said. "It's how I feel."

"Well, as your guardian my decision is final," Alfred said. "We won't return to Gotham until next month, as we'd originally planned, and that's final."

As you'd *originally planned*, Bruce thought, and he still wasn't happy about the situation. He felt as if the monster crisis was partly his doing. After all, if he hadn't launched an all-out quest to bring the Wayne killers to justice, Hugo Strange's atrocities might never have been uncovered. The madman might not have felt the need to accelerate his activities to the point that they ran out of control. Whether this was a realistic viewpoint or not, it was how he *felt*.

That said, he understood that Alfred wasn't being senselessly obtuse. His position came from a place of love and honor.

"I guess we can agree to disagree," Bruce said finally. "I don't agree with your position, but I do respect it."

"Very well then," Alfred said. "Fancy a game of chess? Make it three out of five?"

"I've already beaten you three times in a row."

Alfred's jaw dropped slightly as he realized this was true. "Right then," he said. "Then how about best of seven? If I have another scotch, you're guaranteed to win."

"I think I could beat you regardless," Bruce said.

"Sounds like fighting words to me." Alfred smiled. "Might as well have the scotch anyway then."

He poured another drink, then sat at the table where they kept the antique ivory chess set, the pieces already in place. Bruce had used this set to play with his parents many times before, but rather than upsetting him, these memories seemed comforting.

Only a handful of moves into the game, Bruce employed his queen.

"Checkmate."

Alfred's stunned gaze was priceless.

"Bloody hell," he said. "How'd you do that?"

Bruce laughed, enjoying the time with his best friend.

He still would rather have been fighting monsters in Gotham.

The next morning, Bruce and Alfred arrived at the public ski resort. Although they could've skied at one of the many private resorts in the area, Bruce detested elitism and didn't enjoy flaunting his wealth.

Though he had been born into a wealthy family, it didn't mean he deserved better treatment than anyone else. His experience with Selina and the other street kids, living in the underbelly of Gotham, had reinforced this view. Sometimes his financial situation felt like more of a burden than an asset.

"Looks like we'll have the slopes to ourselves," Alfred said.

As he steered their old Mercedes into the lot, Bruce noticed that there were indeed many fewer cars in the lot than usual, probably since it was a Wednesday—a school and work day for most people in the area.

"We'll have a few good runs," Alfred continued, "then get you back to the chalet and studying for your chemistry exam tomorrow."

A tutor came to the chalet three days a week to keep

Bruce up on his course work. When they returned to Gotham next month, Bruce would return to school at the Anders Academy, and Alfred was determined that he didn't fall behind while they were "across the pond."

They changed in the locker room, and then got in line and bought lift tickets. Behind them, Bruce noticed a man about Alfred's age, with dirty blond hair. He looked Scandinavian, perhaps Swedish. When the man saw Bruce noticing him, he looked away quickly.

"I reckon conditions are nigh perfect today," Alfred said. "Couldn't have ordered better weather." Outside several skiers blissfully slalomed down the bottom of the trail. It was a perfect day for skiing—bright sunshine, light wind, fresh snowfall. After purchasing their tickets, they got in the short line for the ski lift.

"Let's go all the way to the top," Bruce suggested.

"The top of the mountain?" Alfred said. "This is one of the highest peaks in the Alps. There's practically a straight drop near the top, and only professional skiers can get down it without taking a massive spill."

"Are you afraid?" Bruce asked. He was reasonably certain Alfred had done it before.

"No," Alfred said. "Just wise enough to know that there's a fine line between adventurous and reckless. To be quite honest, that's a line I've crossed a few too many times in my life, and like a well-trained dog I've learned to tell the difference."

"Well, I'm not afraid of crossing any lines," Bruce said. "Come on, my skiing has improved every day, and my dad always told me that someday I could go to the top. I think I'm up for the challenge."

Alfred stared at him for a moment, his expression unreadable,

"Fine," he said. "I won't be the one to hold you back. The worst thing that could happen is you break a few bones, maybe have to take a trip to the hospital."

Then Bruce noticed that the blond guy had gotten in line for the lift as well, with four or five people separating them. Once again, he looked right at Bruce, then turned away.

"Alfred, don't make it obvious," Bruce said, keeping his voice low and casual, "but do you see the man with the blond hair, behind us in line?"

Alfred waited a few seconds, then glanced back. He thought he spotted the man Bruce had indicated, though he couldn't be certain.

"Yes, what about him?"

"I saw him in the lodge as well," Bruce said. "It seemed as if he was staring at me."

"Maybe he was looking past you," Alfred said. "That happened to me once, at my local in the East End. I thought this gorgeous woman was staring at me, so I sent a cocktail her way. Turned out she was really staring at the bloke behind me. Worse, she assumed he had sent her the drink. I ate alone that evening."

Bruce looked again, and the fellow was adjusting his gloves. He didn't seem to be aware of Bruce at all.

"Yes, you're probably right."

* * *

They got on the lift and headed to the top of the mountain. The views of seemingly endless white slopes were gorgeous. It seemed so pure, so innocent—the total opposite of Gotham.

It took about twenty minutes to get to the top, and then Bruce and Alfred glided off the lift. A puffy white cloud hovered so close it seemed practically touchable. The snow was so deep that only the tops of the pine trees were visible, like triangles of green amidst all the white.

When they reached the launch point, Bruce had second thoughts about his decision. It was certainly the most difficult trail he'd ever attempted. Parts of the mountain looked so steep, it seemed as if he was about to ski off a cliff.

"Having doubts, are you?"

"No," Bruce lied, trying to sound confident.

Alfred smirked. "Fancy giving me a chance for revenge?"

"Revenge for what?"

"For demolishing me in chess."

"It's not really fair," Bruce said. "You're a much better skier than I am."

"And you're a much better chess player than I am," Alfred said, "but that didn't make me back down from the challenge, did it?"

"Then I accept."

Bruce often felt as if Alfred was testing him—or *training* him—in an attempt to make him become strong, certain, and assertive. Was this one of those times? Maybe

Alfred had only pretended to be apprehensive, knowing that if he resisted, Bruce would insist on going. Well, if that was what Alfred had intended, it had worked.

"Are you ready?" Alfred asked.

"Absolutely," Bruce said.

As they fastened their goggles, the blond guy cut in front of them. Without hesitation, he pushed off and soared down the mountain. A confident, skilled skier, he zipped to the sharp drop then disappeared out of view.

"Okay," Alfred said, "the moment of truth has arrived. On your mark, get set... go!"

By the time Alfred said "go," he was already heading down the mountain.

"Hey," Bruce said, but it was too late.

He pushed off and accelerated on the sharp decline, going from "zero to sixty," as the saying went. The adrenaline rush was amazing. Bruce wasn't sure what he wanted to do with the rest of his life, but he knew he craved this kind of intensity, that he wanted more of it, *needed* more it. But he wouldn't find this sort of stimulation by just running Wayne Enterprises.

Approaching the steepest drop, Bruce braced himself. He was expecting a twenty-foot-or-so drop, and knew he'd catch air. He'd caught air before, and had even gone ski jumping several times with his father, so he knew how to shift his weight forward with the skis lifted upward, to offset the angle of the drop. He got in the proper position.

It wasn't enough to prepare him.

This was more like skiing off a cliff than down a mountain. The drop was about three times what he'd expected, and he didn't know how he could possibly land upright, much less without falling and breaking numerous bones.

Or worse.

Remembering what his father had taught him, he leaned forward so far his head was nearly against the tips of the skis. As he landed, he wedged the skis slightly, like pronating his ankles, but not too much, knowing that if the skis even nicked each other he'd go toppling head-first. At this speed, he could easily die.

He landed like a plane, with the back of the skis touching down first, and then the front. He had never gone this fast before, but somehow he managed to remain upright. Alfred had survived the jump too, and was about twenty feet ahead.

"*Woohoo!*" Bruce called out.

He'd made it past the hardest part of the trail. Although there would be other challenges, he was good on turns and was confident he could handle any other steep areas. Now he could focus on beating Alfred.

Approaching a sharp turn to the right, Bruce gained on his friend. He remained several feet behind him, figuring he'd try to pass on the next straightaway. Alfred knew that Bruce was gaining on him and cut the corner at a sharp angle, forcing Bruce to go wider. That increased his advantage, but they weren't even a third of the way down the mountain yet, and Bruce would have plenty of time to make up ground.

Then, during the next bend, Bruce thought he heard something behind him. He turned his head slightly and saw the blond man skiing about twenty yards back.

How did he get behind *us?*

Bruce made the next turn, then peeked back again and saw that the man had a gun. He fired—apparently at Alfred—though with the noise of the skis gliding along the slope, Bruce could barely hear the gunshot.

"Alfred! Watch out!"

His warning went unheard. They reached a straightaway and Bruce leaned forward, not wedging at all, trying to gain as much speed as possible. He maneuvered alongside his friend. The blond guy might be firing more shots, but Bruce couldn't hear them.

Alfred glanced over.

"He's got a gun!" Bruce yelled.

"What?" Alfred shouted.

"Gun, Alfred! Gun!"

Bruce's right ski must've clipped one of Alfred's because instantly they both went tumbling. Bruce had no control of his body, and occasionally caught a glimpse of Alfred, who also seemed to have no control. Bruce feared they wouldn't stop until they slammed into a tree or another obstruction.

Then, a moment later, everything went whitish gray and he stopped. It took a few moments for it to register that he was in a snow bank. He also realized that he couldn't breathe. Using his arms to push he threw the snow the best he could, and was able to create small opening through which to poke his head.

"Alfred! Where are you? Alfred?" Bruce didn't know if he could free himself, and then he saw he had a worse problem.

The blond man was skiing toward him and Bruce had no way to defend himself. Was this how he was going to die? On a ski slope in the Alps? He flashed back to the alley in Gotham—the night his parents were murdered. He could hear the gunshots, see the blood and his mother's pearls clattering along the cobblestones.

He couldn't die today. It wasn't his time.

The blond man came to a stop. "Where's your friend?" He spoke English with a British accent.

"I don't know," Bruce said. "What do you want?"

The guy smiled, but it wasn't really a smile. It was more a sinister smirk.

"I'll show you what I want."

He aimed the gun. Buried in snow, unable to defend himself in any way, Bruce braced for the pain and eternal darkness.

But the guy didn't shoot him. He turned to his left, looking toward the top of the mountain, where a ski patrol officer had just cut the turn and was speeding toward them. The officer was probably responding to the gunfire.

The blond man took off and sped down the slope. The officer skidded to a stop next to Bruce. He pulled up his black ski mask and said something in German. Bruce knew a little German, but not enough to hold a conversation.

"That man shot at us," Bruce said in English.

The officer nodded, took out a walkie-talkie, and spoke in German. The only word Bruce understood was *"berg"*—mountain. Then the man turned back to Bruce.

"Do you know the man?" He spoke with a heavy German accent.

"No. I have no idea who he was," Bruce said. "But maybe my friend does."

"What friend?"

At that moment Alfred pushed his head out through the snow bank. His face was bright pink and he gasped for breath.

"Oh, bloody hell," he said. Then he noticed the ski patrol officer. "What did I miss?"

The officer dug Bruce out of snow, and then they both helped Alfred. Neither had their skis, which had come loose during the spill.

"Do you know who the guy was?" Bruce asked.

"I didn't get a good look at him," Alfred admitted.

"He was in his twenties maybe," Bruce said. "He had blond hair."

"That description doesn't exactly ring a bell," Alfred said with a hint of sarcasm.

"He had a British accent," Bruce said. "He was after you. I think I was just collateral damage."

"What is that?" the officer asked, confused by the term.

"He wanted to kill him," Bruce said.

"Do you have any enemies?" the officer asked Alfred.

"That's a long conversation, I'm afraid," Alfred replied.

"Hopefully my associates below will capture the man," the officer said. "I will recover your skis."

"Thank you," Bruce said. "Much appreciated. And thank you for coming along when you did. You saved my life."

"I was just doing my job," the officer said. He made certain they were both intact, and once he was satisfied, he skied off. Bruce watched him glide away.

"That must feel so cool," he said. "He has a noble profession, saving people's lives, and it's thrilling as well."

"Well, I'm sure every day isn't as eventful for him as this one," Alfred said.

"Still," Bruce said. "It must feel good."

"No doubt, but more to the point, how are you?" Alfred said. "Did you hurt anything?"

"Nothing that won't heal."

"It's good to be young," Alfred said, wincing as he shifted his neck from side to side.

"Do you have any idea who it was?" Bruce asked.

"I have a theory," Alfred said, "but for both of our sakes, let's hope it's incorrect."

"I told you," Bruce said.

Alfred appeared confused. "Told me what, Master Bruce?"

"That coming to Switzerland was a mistake. We'd both be safer in Gotham."

ELEVEN

At nine o'clock in the evening, Selina arrived at the railway overpass in The Void, one of the worst parts of Gotham. Because of all the crime in The Void, most stayed away from the area, but Selina wasn't most people. Besides, she really was good at getting in and out of places unseen and staying away from dangerous people. Call it her super power.

What the hell? There was nobody at the meeting spot. Not even any cars. Were these guys stupid enough to try to screw her over? If they did, Selina would call in a favor from Fish Mooney. The boss guy and the rest of his crew would be sorry.

A car pulled up and parked just outside the overpass. It was pretty dark here, with only some light from nearby lampposts, so Selina couldn't tell who was in it. Then a woman got out and approached her. At first, Selina couldn't figure out what the woman could be doing there, and she even wondered if the woman was a cop. Was this some kind of setup, like a whatchamacallit, sting operation?

She was about to bolt, but then the woman began to look familiar. Yeah, it was her—the manager lady from the bank. Selina remembered her nametag—"Clarissa Morgan, Bank Manager." She was good with details like that. Her eyes were like camera lenses.

So she was right. The bank manager was involved in this too—the crew had somebody working on the inside. Still, it was kind of surprising that a stuck-up-looking lady like her had gotten mixed up in a bank robbery, much less one with freakin' *monsters*. This woman didn't look like she had a dark side. Then again, Bruce Wayne didn't look like he had a dark side either, and yet Selina knew that deep down, Bruce was as dark as her—maybe darker.

Sometimes what you see with people isn't necessarily what you get.

The woman stopped several feet away. Selina wasn't going to talk first. What was that old saying? *The one who speaks first, loses?* Well, Selina Kyle sure as hell wasn't a loser.

"Wow, it's you," Morgan finally said. "The girl."

"Brilliant observation."

"I'm just surprised, that's all." Morgan said. "How did somebody like you get mixed up in all this?"

"Seriously?" For some reason, Selina thought that was an insult. "Actually, I was thinking of asking you the exact same question."

"Well, I asked it first."

"Well, I'm not answering it first."

That was the way—put it right back on her. Like she was going to tell this lady anything? Yeah, right. For all she knew, the woman was wired, working for Harvey Bullock.

"I was just surprised when I saw you involved with this," Morgan said. "A pretty, tough-looking girl like you. I'd think you'd be smart enough to stay out of trouble."

"Hey, Harvey," Selina said. "How's it going?"

"What?" Morgan sounded totally confused. Or maybe she was just *acting* totally confused.

"The cops have you wired," Selina said. "What did they do, offer you some kind of 'get out of jail free' pass?"

"I'm not wired," Morgan said. "You can check me if you want." She held out her hands. Selina patted her down, but didn't find anything.

"Fine," Selina said. "Then, to answer your question, maybe I don't *want* to stay out of trouble. Maybe I like trouble."

"That's a sad way to live your life. What do your parents have to say about this?"

"I don't have any parents."

"You're an orphan. Even sadder."

"Whoa," Selina said. "Whoever said anything about me being sad? I'm the happiest person I know."

"That in itself is sad."

Oh, for crap's sake, Selina thought.

"Yeah, and where do you come off so high and mighty?" she said. "You helped put the money in the duffel bag this afternoon. If you think I'm sad, you're even sadder. I'm a teenager, I'm allowed to do messed-up stuff. These are my, what do they call 'em, rebellious years. You're an adult—you should know better."

That had hit home like an uppercut to the gut.

"There were extenuating circumstances," Morgan protested.

"That makes it sooo much better," Selina said, smiling. "Tell the judge that before you get sentenced. I bet it'll really get the floodgates going." She continued smiling, pleased with herself.

Morgan remained stoic.

"What's taking them so long anyway?" she asked. "You think they're going to show up?"

"How do I know?" Selina said. "I look like a psychic?"

"Aren't you concerned?"

"No, I know I'm gonna get my money."

"How do you know that?"

"You got a lot of questions, don't you, lady?"

Another car was approaching, the ultra-bright halogen headlights making Selina squint. It came to stop next to Morgan's.

"Looks like our friends finally showed up to the party," Selina said.

"Thank God," Morgan said. "Maybe this nightmare will be over soon."

Yeah, you just go on thinking that. Selina wished she had a dollar for every time she'd heard uppity people like Clarissa Morgan waiting for the nightmare in Gotham to end. *Hello, people.* This nightmare wasn't ending anytime soon.

The two guys got out of the car, followed by the

two monsters. Walking side by side, they approached Morgan and Selina. In the tunnel, with the light behind them, they looked like four black shadows.

"Why did they bring them?" Morgan asked.

"You mean why did the men bring the monsters, or why did the monsters bring the men?" Selina responded.

Morgan didn't answer.

The group stopped several feet in front of them.

"Ladies," the short, scruffy guy said. "How are you this evening?"

Now Selina could see their faces, but she was more concerned about what was missing. They weren't carrying anything.

"Where's my money?" she asked.

"That's a rude reply," the scruffy guy said. "The nice thing to say is, 'I'm fine, thanks, how are you?'"

"I never said I was nice."

"Listen to her," the scruffy guy said. "Now she's sounding like my ex-wife." The guys had a good laugh. It echoed in the tunnel. The monsters just stood there, glaring. The dog-faced one drooled.

Ewww…

"Did you bring our money or not?" Morgan asked.

The men suddenly stopped laughing. For a couple of moments the tunnel was silent.

"First of all," the scruffy guy said, ignoring the question, "I want to congratulate you two for a job well done. That was one of the best heists I ever pulled off. It went without a hitch."

"Without a hitch?" Selina said. "What're you

smoking? You killed a cop and a whole bunch of other people too."

"That's called collateral damage—casualties," the guy said. "You know why that word has 'casual' in it? Cause it don't mean anything. It's not part of the big picture. The big picture is that we came away with a big score. We won—that's all that matters."

Selina was tired of listening to this guy's crap.

"You got our money or not? 'Cause I'm connected to Fish Mooney, so if you mess with me, you're messing with Fish."

"Fish Mooney?" the scruffy guy said. "You think we're scared of her?"

"That's a good one," the tall guy said.

"Fish Mooney's washed up," the scruffy guy said. "She was dead for god's sake."

"Like you said, *was*," Selina replied. "She's back, and stronger than ever. She's got a new crowd."

"Oooh, a crowd," the scruffy guy said. "Now I'm so scared I'm trembling. A back-from-the-dead chick is gonna come after me if I don't pay you."

"So are you planning to give us our money or not?" Morgan asked. Selina rolled her eyes. She hated being in the same boat with such an amateur.

"No," the scruffy guy said, "I'm afraid that's not gonna happen. You two are what we in the business call 'loose ends.'" He turned toward the monsters, then said, "Sic 'em!"

Oh, shit.

Selina was about to flee, or at least try to flee, but

she stopped herself. The monsters weren't attacking. They were looking at each other, smiling a little.

What the hell?

Suddenly agitated, the scruffy guy said, "What're you waiting for, you idiots? I said, sic 'em." Then they moved.

Instead of attacking the two women, the monsters tackled the men. Selina had seen too many gruesome murders to count, but these were unlike anything she'd ever seen—even at the bank. The two men were literally torn to shreds. Limbs went flying, and there was blood everywhere.

Despite all of the bloodshed, Selina was more surprised than horrified. And she had questions. Why were monsters killing their own people? Was this a double-cross, or were they just going psycho for the hell of it?

Morgan wailed like a scream queen in the worst horror movie ever, and it sounded even more bloodcurdling echoing off the walls of the overpass. Selina, meanwhile, didn't make a peep. From growing up on the streets, she knew that panicking was the worst thing she could possibly do. No one could think when their mind was all messed up.

The only problem, Selina quickly realized, was that staying calm wasn't going to help. Not in this screwed-up situation. Did it matter if a little fish was calm when a big shark was about to swallow it whole?

So she took off, heading out of the tunnel and away from the carnage. Then her eyes went wide.

What the hell?

There was a guy running in the opposite direction, toward her.

No, it can't be...

She slowed for maybe a second.

"Jim Gordon, no way." What the hell was he doing here? While she hadn't seen him in months, this wasn't exactly the right time to catch up. So she kept running, clambered up a couple of milk crates, then jumped a six-foot-high fence. She landed on her feet and kept going at a sprint.

When she was about a mile away, she slowed, feeling safe. Then Selina assessed her situation. She couldn't walk back to Central Gotham from here, and there wasn't a lot of street traffic to hitch a ride. She knew an easy way back though. At the railroad tracks, she waited by the bend for a few minutes until the next train came by. The train slowed to take the curve safely, making it easy for Selina to run alongside it then hop on board.

TWELVE

Twenty minutes later Selina walked out of North Station. It wasn't as crowded as it used to be, thanks to the crisis. More were staying home, only going out if they absolutely had to. She walked about five blocks to The Sirens, the new club run by Barbara Kean and Tabitha Galavan.

As always, the club was jumping. It was the new, hip place where Gothamites with money came to spend, and high-end criminals came to make deals and contacts. Barbara, in a tight black leather dress, was having a drink at the bar when she saw Selina enter. Her expression brightened as she got right up and came over.

"Hey, girlfriend," Barbara said, "how've you been?"

Kean looked amazing for a woman who, not long ago, had been an inmate at Arkham. Her short blond hair was styled perfectly, and those diamond earrings looked like the real deal. Like a lot of crazy people Selina knew, Barbara smiled a lot, but she didn't smile the way normal people did when something funny happened. Barbara's sly smile was permanent, like there was a joke being told in her head all the time, but only she got the punch line.

"As good as always," Selina said.

"Hope you're staying out of trouble." Barbara laughed that laugh. "Who'm I kidding? Staying out of trouble isn't fun at all."

"Staying out of trouble has never been a problem for me."

"Well, then I guess I should say, 'lucky you,'" Barbara said. "So what brings you to this neck of the woods?"

"I'm looking for Fish Mooney," Selina said. "Word is she hangs out around here and at a condemned house down in The Void. This is a lot nicer." *And a lot safer too*, Selina thought.

"Maybe you're not so lucky after all," Barbara said. "I've never even met her. If I was a betting woman, though, I'd say you could find her at Falsettos. It's right around the—"

"I know where it is," Selina said abruptly, then she added, "Thanks."

"My pleasure." Barbara smiled, then she got a look on her face. "You know, we should work together again sometime. I have some exciting projects lined up that you'd be a perfect fit for."

"My ears are always open," Selina said.

"Love it." Barbara hugged her. "You'll see. Good times are coming for girls like us."

Selina liked the idea of working with Barbara again.

It might be another opportunity to cash in and move ahead. It was like her life was a maze—she knew where she was going, she just had to figure out how to get there.

Falsettos was a "hidden club," like an old speakeasy, with the entrance in the back of a sneaker store. It wasn't hidden because it was trendy and cool. No, there was no velvet rope at Falsettos, just a lot of ex-cons and criminals hiding from the law.

As Selina entered the sneaker store, Sammy—the owner who was, like, ninety years old—came over and headed her off.

"What can I do for you?"

"It's me, Selina."

Sammy squinted. "Who?"

"Selina," she said. "Selina Kyle. The girl who used to tip you off, tell you where the delivery trucks were parked. Without me you wouldn't have any stock for your"—she glanced around wryly—"shoe store."

His expression brightened. "Oh, the street kid. *Selina*—that's right. Come on, come in, come in. What can I get for you?" He glanced down toward her boots. "Need some sneakers?"

"I'm looking for Falsettos."

One cool thing about Sammy—he didn't give her any crap like asking for ID. Though the fact that he could barely see her probably helped.

"Straight through," he said.

"Thanks," Selina said. "By the way, do you know if Fish Mooney's in there?"

"Who?"

"Fish Mooney." This was getting old. "Yeah, yeah, she's in there." Sammy still seemed confused though. "Enjoy, enjoy."

Selina went behind the back counter and down a short hallway. As soon as she opened the door she could hear—and feel—the pulsing beat. Squinting while her eyes adjusted, she passed through the dark, seedy club. In contrast to the empty store, it was surprisingly crowded back here. There had to be at least thirty people hanging around, drinking and smoking. There were probably some monsters in here too she figured. Made sense if this was a Fish Mooney hangout.

Moving further into the club, she didn't see anyone she recognized, especially not Fish. It was more than possible that Sammy had gotten it wrong though, as he definitely wasn't playing with a full deck. Selina was about to give up and leave when she spotted her old boss.

Fish was in the back of the club, sitting comfortably on a couch talking to a big, tough-looking guy with slicked-back hair. He might as well have had a sign on his forehead.

Gangster.

Deciding to leave well enough alone and come back later, she started to edge back out, but then Fish spotted her and waved at her to come over.

"Well, well, Selina Kyle, my old prodigy," Fish said.

"I'm just finishing some business here, why don't you join us?"

"Are you sure?" Selina said. "'Cause I can—"

"Positive."

At first glance Fish's eyes looked freaky, but kind of cool too. One was brown, the other a vibrant blue. From what Selina had heard, the blue one was the replacement for an eye Fish had plucked out herself. Just the thought made her wince.

A lot of people couldn't pull off the "one blue eye look," but Fish Mooney could.

Selina sat in a chair across from them. The guy didn't acknowledge her, or even look at her. He seemed totally mesmerized by Fish.

"So it's agreed. You'll bring me fifty percent of your gambling revenue every week, indefinitely."

"Yes, Ms. Mooney.

"Very well then." Fish reached across the table and held the man's hand. Selina stared as a glowing green light appeared where she was touching him. She'd heard that Fish had escaped from Arkham with some weird mind-control ability, but she'd never seen it for herself.

"You're dismissed," Fish said to the man.

Obediently, he got up and left.

"Well, that's something you don't see every day," Selina said, trying to keep it casual. In fact, she was impressed as hell and wished she could do that too.

"Ha, speaking the truth," Fish said. "Well, as you can see, I have people under my thumb—no pun intended. So how've you been? You're staying alive anyway, which is more than I can say for myself."

"I'm getting by," Selina replied.

"That doesn't make it sound like you're getting where you want to be," Fish said, peering intently at her. "At least not as fast as you want to get there. If I were you, I'd seriously consider a smart career move... like working with me."

Wow, another job offer? Selina thought. *Guess it's my lucky day.* She kept it out of her expression though.

"I don't know," Selina said. "I mean, that didn't work out so well last time."

"Define 'not so well.'"

"You got killed, for one thing."

"Just a technicality, as you can see. I'm telling you, Selina, our glory days are coming back. I mean, just look what happened to Gotham in my absence. There's been mayhem, destruction, chaos. A mayor was murdered, a madman almost triggered a nuclear explosion. I'm telling you, it's up to us to provide some sanity for this city."

"You've got that right," Selina said, and she tilted her head. "You've always believed in me, too, and every girl needs a role model." She was lying like hell of course. There was only one person she totally trusted—Bruce Wayne. He'd never lied to her, and he never would. Hell, she wasn't sure he knew *how* to.

Besides, something had changed about Fish since she had come back to life, and that made Selina wary. It wasn't just the green light power. Something about her thinking had changed too—something about the way she acted. Who knew what else Hugo Strange had done to her?

"All right, enough of the ass kissing," Fish said. "Come clean. What are you here for, except to remind me how amazing I am?"

"I need your help," Selina said.

"I'm shocked," Fish said sarcastically. "What with?"

"A couple of monsters owe me money."

"Monsters? What monsters?"

Selina told her all about the robbery, how the monsters had been involved, and what had happened under the overpass. Fish listened without any expression until Selina got to the part about the fight in the tunnel. Then she interrupted.

"I'm sorry you had to see that."

The comment seemed strange, and Fish didn't seem surprised that the monsters had torn up the men. But why was she was concerned that Selina had seen it? Okay, yeah, Selina did see her as sort of a twisted mother figure, but it was still weird to hear Fish Mooney sounding so motherly.

"Oh, and when I was leaving, something else happened," Selina said. "Jim Gordon ran past me and into the tunnel."

"Reallllly?" Fish said, dragging out the word.

"Yeah," Selina replied. "I mean, I'd heard he's hunting monsters, so that's probably why he was there. What else could it be?"

"Did he kill the monsters or capture them?"

"I don't know," Selina said. "I was running away in

the other direction. Why do you want to know?"

Fish seemed distracted for a few seconds, then she snapped out of it. "Well, you want your money from the robbery, don't you? If Jim Gordon has it, I can help you get it back." Meaningfully she tapped her thumb against her fingers and smiled.

"That would be awesome."

"How long ago did this happen?" Fish asked.

"I dunno. Like an hour ago, maybe a little more. I came right here."

"That's enough time," Fish mused. "If Jim Gordon killed those monsters, I would've heard about it already. Chances are they got away."

"So will you help me get my money?"

"How about we make a deal?" Fish said. "I get your money, and *then* you come work for me. Sounds like a win-win situation for you."

Selina mulled it over. It was what she wanted—to work for Fish again. But Fish was acting kind of... off. This wasn't the person she had known before.

What the hell, she thought. *It's not like I've got anything better to do. If it gets weird, I'll just take off.*

"Sure," she said. "Why not?"

Fish looked right into Selina's eyes, then reached across the table and tried to hold her hand. Before she could touch her, Selina yanked her hand away. Fish shot her a look, then seemed to chill out.

"It's okay," she said. "You have nothing to worry about. I just wanted to shake your hand to close our deal, and get your guarantee that nothing discussed at this table *leaves* this table."

"I've heard about what you've been doing to people," Selina said, "controlling their minds. Well, nobody controls *my* mind. You'll just have to take my word for it."

"That's my savvy girl." Fish grinned. "It's why I like you and, more importantly, it's why I *trust* you. You're right—you and I don't need handshakes, do we? We have an unspoken promise between us. I know I'll always have your loyalty, and I hope you know you have mine."

Selina didn't believe her because she didn't fully believe anyone—even her closest friends.

"I know I do," she said.

"You and I can go a long, long way together," Fish said. "In some ways, you remind me of a young me. In other words, you got it goin' on, girl. Our future has never been so bright."

Smiling, Selina stood up to leave.

"Oh, and one more thing," Fish said. "If you happen to run into Jim Gordon again, contact me immediately, and let me know where he is. The sooner, the better."

"What do you want from Gordon?"

"He may have information about the monsters that could be… useful," Fish said. "Just be sure to call me as quickly as you can."

"Will do," Selina, said, then she turned and walked away, feeling Fish Mooney's gaze burning into the back of her head. Especially that one vivid blue eye.

As she was leaving Falsettos, she stopped dead

and moved off to one side, trying to blend in. Another woman was arriving. She was dressed in heels and a flowing dress that had probably been pretty before it had gotten blood all over it. She had bruises all over her arms and face. Yet none of that was what grabbed Selina's attention.

This woman had four ears.

Selina reminded herself that it was none of her business. It was probably a normal thing these days, a monster hanging out in a speakeasy. Besides, she wasn't an idiot. She knew Fish was looking for Jim Gordon for a reason, probably to kill him. This was probably connected.

"Tuck!" Fish said from the back of the room. "Girl, you're a real mess."

No, it wasn't any of Selina's business. In Gotham you had to put yourself first and forget about everyone else.

It was the only way to survive.

THIRTEEN

After the incident with the bikers outside of Donny's Diner, Gordon's cop instincts kicked in. It wasn't something he could just turn off. Clarissa *had* to be hiding something. This was far more than just grief, and most likely it had to do with the bank robbery. If that was the case, she had to be in way over her head.

He could've ignored his instincts, gone on with his new career. After all, there were a lot more monsters on his list, and he had more leads to follow than hours in the day. He'd already gone out of his way to help her, and if she didn't want any more help, he had to take "no" for an answer, right?

To hell with that.

When Clarissa drove out of the parking lot, Gordon got in his car. He counted to ten to give her a little head start, and then he followed her.

Maybe it was a bad idea, but Gordon couldn't bring himself to let her get in any deeper. Besides, he told himself, the bank robbery was unsolved, and Clarissa might lead him to the robbers. While bringing robbers to justice wasn't part of his job description anymore, these robbers hung around with monsters—and monsters *were* in his job description.

That certainly justified the effort. If the robbers happened to end up in jail in the process, so much the better. It was no skin off his nose.

Once a cop, always a cop.

Damn it.

Gordon followed her onto the South End Expressway. There were several cars between them so he didn't think she realized she was being tailed. She bypassed most of Gotham and seemed to be heading out of town, then she suddenly turned onto an exit ramp leading into The Void, one of the seediest areas in town.

To get over to the right lane in time, Jim had to practically cut off a tractor-trailer, forcing the driver to screech the brakes. Fortunately, Clarissa had already turned off the ramp onto a surface road, and probably wasn't aware of the disturbance Jim had caused.

He was surprised that Clarissa was heading toward The Void. Gordon had been there several times in an official capacity, and more recently because the lawless environment made it an ideal location for monsters who wanted to lie low. It had the reputation of being a place where even cops were afraid to go. While the rumors had never scared him, there had been cases of people—including cops—going missing here. Passing junkyards piled with debris and burnt-out lots proved to Gordon, beyond a doubt, that she didn't know what she was doing. There was no way a woman like her would head into an area like this unless she absolutely had to.

"You're definitely not heading home," he said out loud. He followed her for another half a mile or so and, if anything, the neighborhood became worse, huge barren lots and empty shells of buildings, like a war zone. Occasionally he saw fires burning in the depths of the blackness, or in shantytowns among the ruins.

Finally, Clarissa parked at the entrance to a railroad overpass. Gordon stopped his car well behind her, next to an overgrown lot, then killed the lights. He got out of the car, being careful to close the door quietly, and hid in the underbrush to stay out of view. It almost felt like the old days, on a stakeout, except here he didn't have anyone watching his back.

Clarissa got out of her car and headed into the tunnel-like area, where there was someone waiting. He couldn't see who the other person was, but the silhouette looked familiar, like…

Selina Kyle? Yeah, it was her all right. Although Gordon had to be about fifty feet away, that short curly hair and cocky posture were dead giveaways.

Selina Kyle was a magnet for trouble, and somehow Clarissa had been drawn to her. That couldn't be good, but did it mean that Selina had been involved in the robbery as well? It seemed like something out of her league. Besides, she was basically a good kid. She sure as hell didn't seem like someone who would be involved with monsters. There had to be another factor in play.

A missing link.

Bingo! Maybe this is the missing link.

Gordon ducked further into the brush as a car with its brights on passed by. When it came to a stop, four guys got out. Cancel that—two guys and two monsters. Jim recognized the monsters right away. They were both on his list. The tall, multi-colored one supposedly went by the name "Marino." He had a rep as one of the most dangerous monsters in Gotham and had been linked to more than a dozen homicides. He liked to rip the arms off of his victims.

The shorter monster went by the name "The Dog," and for ridiculously obvious reasons. Also particularly violent, The Dog had killed or assaulted more than twenty people over the past several months, selecting his targets indiscriminately. Together they made a particularly deadly duo. Capturing them both would be a huge coup.

Why did the short human look familiar? Gordon knew he'd seen him somewhere before, and it wasn't in church.

This had to be the crew that had robbed Gotham Federal, but something still didn't make sense. What were two of the most dangerous Arkham escapees doing hanging out with a couple of humans? Monsters simply didn't associate with humans—if anything, most of them kept as far away from people as they could. Sure, there were some—like Gordon's doppelganger—who attempted to assimilate into the human population, but not many could pull it off. The majority usually hung out with other monsters, or remained lone wolves.

Gordon's flip phone rang. *Ugh*, he hadn't turned the volume off. Luckily, it was very low, not loud enough for anyone to hear, but it wasn't a mistake he would've made when he was a cop.

"Yeah?" he whispered.

"Jim?" Bullock said. "That you? I can barely hear you."

"Sort of in the middle of something right now."

"What?"

"I said I'm in the middle of something," he said, a notch louder.

"Hopefully it's some lady action," Bullock said. "Sorry to interrupt, but this is important."

"What is it?"

"You want the bad news or the bad news?"

"I'll take the bad news."

"So our guys went down to that spot where you said you took down Nip and Tuck, the building with the lamppost."

"So?" Gordon said. "How's that bad news?"

"Tuck's gone."

"I knew she was dead. So what?"

"No, I mean she *escaped*."

"What? But I saw their bodies. That chandelier had to weigh a couple of hundred pounds."

"Don't know what to tell ya, Jim. These monsters, they're tough cookies. The impact was enough to kill

Nip—we shoveled him away to the morgue already—but Tuck's missing in action."

He couldn't believe it. Gordon knew what he'd seen. Still, he should've stuck around until the officers got there. He'd been working long hours lately, and hadn't been in the best headspace. He had to give himself a pass. It wasn't like he could do anything about it now.

"I'll find her."

"No offense, but I hope we beat you to it," Bullock said. "I got a monster scorecard I gotta fill too. So who's the rebound chick?"

"What?"

"The one you're rebounding with," Bullock said. "More power to ya, my friend. When you get kicked off the horse, you gotta get back on before you forget how to ride."

"Gotta go, Harv, check in with you later."

"Happy trails," Bullock said.

Gordon ended the call.

He focused all of his attention on the conversation in the train overpass, straining to hear what they were saying, and failing. He felt some trepidation. Taking on monsters was hard enough, but the men were likely armed. This was a crazy situation for him to address alone. If he was still a cop, he'd have a SWAT team backing him up. Those days were in the past though. If Gordon wanted to make a living as a bounty hunter, he had to do it on his own.

Releasing the safety on his gun, he crouched and

waited, ready to make his move. Then something strange happened.

The short guy seemed to become upset about something. He started shouting, then the monsters suddenly attacked the men. It happened so fast Gordon didn't have the chance to react even if he had wanted to. Now, as the scene played out, he scanned for Clarissa and Selina.

The monsters attacked the men like total savages. The big one, Marino, grabbed the taller guy, ripping an arm off and actually *beating* him with it. The Dog jumped on the shorter thug, ripping a chunk out of his shoulder with one bite. Within just a few seconds, the monsters had literally chewed up and spat out the men.

Clarissa and Selina would be next. Leaving the undergrowth at a sprint, he charged toward the tunnel. As he did, Selina came running in his direction. When she saw him, she slowed, just for a moment.

"Jim Gordon, no way."

Then she continued her escape. Gordon was glad she was on her way to safety. That meant he only had one person to worry about.

Sure enough the monsters, dripping with blood, were eyeing Clarissa like she was their next victim. They moved to either side of her, and The Dog grabbed her, cutting into her with his claws. She tried to scream, but all that came out was a breathy wail.

"Hey, leave her alone!" Gordon shouted.

He began firing at the taller monster.

Marino took several slugs with a loud grunt. He

howled and gestured to his companion, and the monsters fled, dashing toward the parked car that had brought them there. Gordon continued to charge toward them with gun blazing. They dove into the car, it growled to life, and they drove away.

Gordon didn't think any of his bullets had injured them all that much. Unlike their victims, however, he had been ready for them, and that was enough to send them running.

Gordon went over to Clarissa where she had fallen to her knees. She seemed dazed, clearly in shock, and she was bleeding badly from her arms. Some blood soaked through the front of her blouse as well.

"What..." She looked up at him. "What are you doing here?"

"I figured you might be in danger." He looked around the tunnel at the scattered bloody body parts, and it was hard to tell that the victims had even been human. "I thought it was something bad, but I didn't think it was this bad. Come on, we have to get you to a hospital."

"No, I can't go to a hospital," she said. "I'll get arrested."

"Would you rather die?"

"Leave," she said. "I don't need you, and you don't have to keep showing up, saving me. I'm not some damsel in distress."

"I don't know about the damsel part, but you seemed to be in a hell of a lot of distress. If I didn't show up, you'd be scattered around here like your friends."

"They're not…" She corrected herself. "They *weren't* my friends, and maybe that wouldn't be such a bad thing anyway." As if suddenly realizing something, she lurched to her feet and looked around frantically in every direction. "Wait, where did they go? Did they leave? Did they take the money?"

"So that's why you came here," Gordon said, "to get your share of the money from the robbery."

"But they didn't give it to us," she said. "The monsters have the money now. We have to go after them. You don't understand. I *need* that money."

"We'll take you to the hospital, then we'll worry about the monsters."

"No," Clarissa said. "*Please.*"

"You're coming with me," he said in a no-nonsense tone. "Listen, we don't have to go to a hospital. I've stitched myself up before, I can stitch you up too. Let's go." He grabbed her arm, careful to avoid the bleeding wound, and led her back to her car.

"Can you drive?" Gordon asked. "You can't leave your car here—at the scene of a double homicide." She nodded, and he helped her into the car. "How's that?" he asked.

"Fine, I think." She didn't sound very convincing, but it would have to do.

"I'm going to get my car, and when I drive by, follow me," he instructed. "Don't get any ideas about taking off. Your best chance of finding those monsters is sticking with me." She seemed calmer now, and she listened to him intently.

"Why?" she asked. "What do you know about monsters?"

"There's no time for that now—we need to get you someplace where I can stop the bleeding and patch you up." He looked her over again, then added, "Let's just say that as a former detective, there's a lot more I can do for you than you can do for yourself." That would have to be enough.

"Fine," she said finally. "Lead the way."

FOURTEEN

Gordon lived in a small basement studio apartment in Gotham's North Village. It wasn't exactly like the swanky, high-end apartment he'd lived in before he went to prison. He'd had to give up the lease on that place, and as an ex-con with a wiped credit history and no salaried job, it had been hard to find anyplace willing to rent to him.

Luckily he knew Carlos, the landlord of the building, and Carlos owed him a favor. Last year, armed robbers had broken into Carlos's apartment, tied up him and his wife, and stolen ten thousand dollars' worth of jewelry. Gordon and Bullock had apprehended the criminals, associates of Carmine Falcone, and recovered everything.

Feeling indebted, Carlos told Gordon that he owed him a favor. As a cop who tried to go by the book, Gordon didn't cash in on favors from civilians. Now that he was a civilian himself, rules like that no longer applied. When he had returned, devastated, from the

Lee debacle down South, he went right to Carlos.

"About that favor…"

When Gordon and Clarissa entered the tiny apartment, he flicked on the light. The room consisted of the kitchen area and the furniture that "came with the apartment"—a single bed, and chewed up couch, and a table with one chair. A couple of large roaches on the kitchen counter scampered away into a crevice.

"Sorry I didn't get a chance to introduce my roommates," Gordon said. Clarissa didn't respond—not even a chuckle. Either his attempt at humor didn't go over well, or she was too out of it to even care. She was pale—almost certainly shock—and unsteady on her feet.

"Sit down," Gordon said.

Clarissa sat in the chair.

He went into the bathroom and returned with a suture kit. As a bounty-hunting bachelor, Gordon rarely had any food in the fridge, but he had a suture kit and lots of bandages and antibiotic ointments.

Bending over her, he peeled back her sleeves.

"Some of these cuts look pretty deep," he said. "It's a good thing I'm doing this. I'm not a pro, but I've gotten a lot of stitches over the years, so I know how it's done. Still, I think it's about fifty-fifty that one of these wounds might get infected." He cleaned out the worst of the gashes on her arm.

"I have to call somebody," Clarissa said.

Gordon began sewing her up.

"It'll have to wait."

"You don't understand," she said. "He could be in trouble."

"Who could be in trouble?"

Clarissa seemed reluctant to answer. "My… fiancé."

"Why would the monsters want to hurt your fiancé?"

"Not the monsters. The loan sharks."

"Excuse me?"

"That's what got me involved in all this," Clarissa said. "My fiancé had debts and I was trying help him."

"So the robbery was your idea?"

"No. Not at all. Eddie knew the guys involved, and they were supposed to have the monsters under control."

"You thought those guys could control the monsters?"

"It seemed like they could when we met. It was supposed to be a routine robbery. They'd get the money, and no one would get hurt. Then that cop got involved, and—"

"That *police officer* was killed," Gordon said harshly. "So were several civilians—innocent bystanders. You have their blood on your hands, whether you like it or not. I'm going to make sure you're brought to justice, but if you do the right thing and help me find those monsters, you might get some leniency in court. Right now that's the best hope you have."

"I don't want to go to jail," she said.

"It doesn't seem like there's any way out of it, but it might not be for long. The important thing right now is to get the monsters off the streets. That will save lives. Those things are vicious psychopaths, just like their creator."

They stopped talking while Gordon continued to tend to her injuries. Occasionally she would gasp, but for the most part she remained silent.

"I want to do what's right," Clarissa said, "and I want to redeem myself any way I can. But what about my fiancé? What about Eddie?"

"I'll tell you what," Gordon said, "if you and your fiancé agree to help us, I can try to get you both into protective custody. Honestly I don't have much pull in the GCPD these days, but I think Captain Bullock would be happy if we got these monsters off the board. Especially if he gets credit for the capture."

"*Ouch*," Clarissa said as Gordon continued to stitch her up.

"Sorry," he said. "I'm almost done."

They went quiet again as he finished the last stitches and tied off the thread. Then he applied some antibacterial gel to each of the wounds—including a few that hadn't been stitched—and began to load everything back into his kit.

"I can't thank you enough for helping me like this. I mean, you've certainly gone out of your way, and I honestly don't know if I would've done the same thing. I mean if I were in your place."

"I guess it's just a habit," he replied.

"Well, there're much worse habits," Clarissa said. "And you were right. I deserve everything that I get. I just loved... *love* my fiancé so much, and even though I know he's bad for me, that I deserve better, I just can't break away from him. I can't expect you to understand that."

"Actually, I know exactly where you're coming from."

"You do?"

"As far as making bad choices? Yeah, I do."

"I never dreamed I'd get involved in anything like this," she said. "I was always the good girl. I didn't rebel, I did well in school. I got a good job, worked my way up, and just wanted to start a family. It seemed like I was on track. I was living a quiet life, with a great career, and a fiancé I was in love with. I thought I had it all. Then I discovered that he had this other life, this secret life I knew nothing about. It was like the person I thought I had fallen in love with didn't actually exist."

"You're not alone," Gordon said. "When somebody plays mind games with you like that, you start to question your own sanity. It makes you feel like *you're* the crazy one, which you start to realize was probably their intention all along." He shut the lid to the kit. "There, we're all done."

"Thank you," Clarissa said, standing. She was still a bit shaky, but was able to steady herself.

Gordon looked around. "I'd offer you something to eat, but I don't have any food."

"How long have you been living here?"

"A few months," he replied. "Haven't had a chance to decorate."

"You'd never guess a bachelor lived here," Clarissa said, a hint of sarcasm in her voice. Gordon took that as a good sign.

"So tell me what you know about the monsters," he said.

"What do you want to know?"

"Do you know where they're staying? How they got involved with the robbery? Any idea what else they may have planned?"

"No, no, and no."

Gordon didn't think she was lying.

"What did the bikers want from you?"

Clarissa looked away. "I can't tell you that."

"Does it have to do with Eddie?"

She didn't answer.

"Look, you've already told me about the debt. I'm trying to help you," he said, "but you have to help yourself. What're you afraid of? Who're you protecting?"

"You can't help me," Clarissa said. "I'm in too deep."

"You're talking to the expert on that," Gordon said. "Give it a shot."

She looked straight at him, conflict playing across her features. Finally, she took a deep breath and let it out slowly.

"Okay, I think Eddie, my fiancé, I think he told those bikers about the robbery. I think they thought I already had my share of the money and wanted to rob me."

"Maybe Eddie set you up himself."

"No, Eddie wouldn't do that. He loves me."

"Some people love money more than people."

"No. No, that's not Eddie." She still looked confused.

"What about the monsters?" Gordon asked.

"I don't think they have anything to do with the bikers, or even the loan sharks," Clarissa said. "I think it's completely separate things. The monsters were with these guys Eddie knows, and I think they just double-crossed the guys."

"Why did they think they could trust monsters?"

"They treated them like they were trained dogs," she replied. "I think they thought they were in control."

"Well, that certainly backfired," Gordon said. "Talk about biting the hand that feeds you." Then he had another thought. "How did Selina get involved in all this?"

"Is that the girl's name?" Clarissa asked. "I hadn't met her until a couple of minutes before you showed up. I saw her in the bank though. Seemed like her whole job had been to lure the guard out of the bank…" She broke down then, falling back into the chair before Gordon could catch her. "You must think I'm an idiot."

"Why do you say that?"

"Because I've risked so much for someone who's so bad for me," she replied, gasping for breath. "It's impossible to explain, unless you've experienced it yourself. I want to get away from him, but I can't. Something about him keeps sucking me back in."

"I was in the same situation once."

"You were?" That seemed to calm her.

"I thought I was in love, and I guess I was. Every time she showed me her true colors, I never wanted to believe it was true. My brain couldn't overrule my heart."

"Yes," Clarissa said. "That's it exactly. How did you get over it?"

Gordon recalled Barbara trying to murder his true love, Leslie. Then how Barbara had been admitted to Arkham as a full-blown mental patient. He twisted his mouth up in an ironic smile.

"Time," he said. "It just takes time."

Clarissa seemed to have recovered from her breakdown. She came to her feet and walked around the messy apartment.

"So now that you're not a cop," she said, "what do you do to earn a living?"

"I, um, just do some consulting."

"What kind of consulting?"

"You know, a little bit of everything," he said. "I also do some, um, security work here and there."

Clarissa picked up a flyer on the kitchen counter, detailing the bounties that had been offered for the monsters. There were other flyers there as well.

"Bounties," she said. "Those things are worth money."

"Yeah," he agreed. "I just picked those up." *Time to change the subject.* "So you sure you're not hungry? I could go across the street to the grocery store and—"

"Wait," Clarissa said. "Is that why you're helping me? Because you want bounties from these monsters, and you thought I knew where they were hiding out?"

He couldn't lie to her, but he smiled a little, trying to soften it.

"Well, I can't say that's not a part of it, but I also didn't want to see you—"

"Unbelievable," Clarissa said, her voice rising. "All that crap about redeeming myself, and how you understand what I'm going through. Coming on like Mr. Supportive, when you couldn't give a *damn* about me. You're just thinking about yourself, like everybody else in this goddamn city."

"I do want to help you," he said.

"Yeah, right." She tried to get to the door, but he blocked her.

"Where're you going?"

"Get out of my way."

"It's a mistake," Gordon said. "Those bikers know who you are. And who knows what the monsters will do. It's not safe for you to be out there alone."

"Yeah, like you care."

"I do care. Whatever else is involved, I do care."

She glared at him.

"Let me go or I'll call the cops."

"You committed a bank robbery today," he said. "You're not calling the cops."

"And you're an ex-con. If I tell the cops you tried to rape me, you'll go right back to prison."

Gordon thought about this. While he knew he could call her bluff—she wasn't likely to call the cops—he also knew there was nothing he could do to stop her. If someone wanted to mess up their life, there was only so much he could do to intervene.

He moved aside to let her pass.

"Good luck with the bounties," she said. "Hope you get rich."

She slammed the door as hard as she could.

FIFTEEN

Monsters. On the whole they were as stupid as they were grotesque. Fish was mortified that she could be identified as one of them.

Technically.

Just because—like Hugo Strange's other... *experiments*—she had been brought back to life and given a new, well, *attribute,* that didn't make her like the savages roaming the streets of Gotham. Fish was superior, and she didn't need any proof or validation. It was a fact, plain and simple.

For one, Fish had intelligence. Not every monster was a moron, but most of them weren't exactly geniuses. Who in Gotham was smarter than Fish Mooney? As demented as he was, Hugo Strange might've rivaled Fish's genius, but look where that got him—he was in custody now, while Fish was free to pursue her own agenda.

Who else was there? Who else possessed the combination of brilliance, cunning, and street smarts, plus the vision to address the big picture?

If anything, Fish was smarter than before she'd died, though it still made her shudder to think of it that way. She was sharper, more focused, and more determined than ever. She had plans—big plans—to take over the underworld of Gotham, and so far those plans were proceeding without a hitch.

Making her work that much easier, there was a power void in Gotham. Salvatore Maroni was dead, and Carmine Falcone had lost most of his influence. Penguin may have thought his time had come, but *think again, Oswald*. Fish's reappearance seemed to have frightened the little man so much that no one had heard a peep from him for weeks. *Poor guy.* No doubt he was still alive, just lying low somewhere, hoping she didn't show up to demand payback.

For the moment at least, Penguin wasn't a genuine concern.

To gain control of the mobs Fish would have to use the monsters to her benefit. Thanks to the ability Hugo Strange had bestowed upon her, they were like putty in her hands, every bit as much as normal human beings. What was more, as much as she loathed them, they saw her as one of their own, and she could employ that to her advantage.

Did controlling the monsters make her feel powerful? *Hell, yeah, baby!* The police department was thoroughly overwhelmed by the monster crisis. *Poor Harvey.* Fish may have liked Bullock—he had a boorish sort of charm—but that didn't mean she cared about him. The GCPD could crash and burn, and all the better. It gave her that much more chance to thrive.

For she'd been operating under the radar. While it seemed as if she was out of the picture, in reality she'd been masterminding much of the chaos in Gotham by controlling the monsters' thoughts and actions. One touch and all she had to do was give them orders, which they obeyed without question. They robbed banks, looted stores, burglarized homes, and Fish got a healthy cut of all the action.

Fish had made more money in recent months than she'd made in the rest of her life combined. Now *that* was coming back from the dead in style.

She'd influenced the monsters involved in the Gotham Federal heist. Those two were mute, and she'd nicknamed them Big Guy and Little Guy, programming them to take orders from Nick Angel and let him think he was in control. In the end she'd given them instructions to kill Nick and everyone else involved in the robbery, then bring her the proceeds.

Nick had screwed Fish on a deal just a few years ago, in Fish's former life. She never forgot that sort of thing, so the murder was both profitable and satisfying on a personal level. She hadn't known, however, that Selina Kyle had been involved in the robbery. The bank manager would need to be eliminated, but what Selina didn't know couldn't hurt her.

Fish had plans for that little kitten.

Tuck and the late Nip had been particularly profitable for Fish, in no small part because they were both so deliciously ruthless. How fortunate that at least one of them had survived. Nip's death, however, revealed a major hindrance in her long-term planning. While the cops hadn't been much of an obstacle, there had been one individual who made life particularly difficult.

James Gordon.

The man had already been shamed out of his job with the police. For a while it seemed as if he'd left town, likely thinking his tribulations wouldn't follow him. Couldn't he just do the smart thing and stay out of Gotham for good? Some people couldn't leave well enough alone—no matter how many times they got knocked down, they just kept coming back for more.

Since setting himself up to make a living on bounties, Gordon had captured or killed some of Fish's best creatures. Though there was only one Jim Gordon, and there were a great many Arkham escapees, he somehow managed to do far more than his share of damage. Fish couldn't just stand by and allow Gordon to thwart her agenda.

To that end, she had leaked the information to Gordon, leading him to Nip and Tuck's hangout. Ricardo had been especially helpful. No doubt he'd held back as long as he could, fearing Fish's wrath, but Gordon had always been very… persuasive.

Even so, the plan had backfired. Instead of killing Gordon, they had let him get the upper hand. That left him active, and he very nearly stopped Big Guy and Little Guy too. That would have cost Fish thousands of dollars.

Enough is enough.

Gordon's bounty hunting career had to end—and she knew exactly who had the motivation to make it happen.

"I'm so sorry about what happened to Nip," Fish said. "I know how much you loved him." The… woman… who sat across from her went tense and the rage in her was apparent. She looked much better than she had the last time she came to Falsettos, cut up and bloody.

"Did you set us up?" Tuck demanded.

Smart question for a dumb monster.

"No, of course not," Fish lied. "Why do you say that?"

"That asshole Gordon had been looking for us for months, and we'd been able to dodge him, no problem. Then he suddenly showed up, after Ricardo DeMonti ratted on us. But how did Gordon find out about DeMonti?"

"How would I know?" Fish said, then her expression went from sincere to deadly serious. "I advise you, however, to choose your words carefully. Remember who you're speaking to. Sympathy only goes so far." As she spoke, Fish reached out and touched the back of Tuck's hand. A subtle green light appeared as she stared into the monster's eyes.

"You'll do as I say, and you'll be loyal."

The fire of rage left Tuck's expression, to be replaced by a flat expression of complacency.

"Yes," she said.

Leaning closer so that their faces were practically touching, and to make sure that there were no misunderstandings, Fish continued. "Go kill Clarissa Morgan," she said. "I'll give you the address. And then kill Jim Gordon. Do you understand?"

"I understand."

"Good. In that case"—Fish let go of her hand—"you're dismissed."

SIXTEEN

Tuck loved killing people. *"It's what you were born to do,"* her creator had told her many times during training. He told her that, *"Killing will make you stronger. Every time you kill someone, their energy will become yours."*

During her time roaming the streets of Gotham, Tuck had killed more people even than Nip, and she felt stronger and stronger because of it. But Strange didn't just teach Tuck how to kill. He taught her how to love. She had been instructed to "love Nip deeply," which she did without hesitation. She and her soul mate were inseparable.

Even when Fish Mooney began to give them instructions, it felt natural. It felt as if Fish was an extension of Strange, that when she gave them orders, it was actually the doctor reaching out to them, with Fish as the medium. Following orders was instinctive, as long as Nip was with her.

Then everything changed.

Nip died right next to her, and it was the worst

moment of Tuck's life. She'd expected to die with him, and when that didn't happen, it seemed wrong. It was as if their very nature had betrayed her. And Tuck was pretty sure nature wasn't the only betrayer.

How had Gordon tracked them down?

This time when Tuck met with Fish, she suspected the woman was lying to her. When Fish touched her, the rage dimmed and the urge to follow orders became overwhelming. Yet a short time later the rage returned, overpowering whatever hold Fish had forced upon her. With the rage, her suspicions returned.

This time she wouldn't be following instructions for the sake of another person. Oh, Tuck planned to accept Fish's orders. She would kill Clarissa Morgan, and then Jim Gordon. *Especially* Gordon. If Tuck discovered that Fish had leaked the information that had led to Nip's death, she would kill Fish too.

Give that bitch what she deserves.

Thanks to her extra ears, Tuck had exceptional hearing. Bred as a hunter, she also knew when she was prey. She knew when someone was approaching her from behind, could hear the breathing and even a heartbeat if the person tried to hide.

Just now she was the predator, walking the short distance from the club to Clarissa Morgan's address. When she arrived she found a nice apartment building in a middle-class downtown neighborhood. There was no doorman, but the door was locked, so Tuck waited for someone to enter or leave the building, then she slipped in behind them.

If this worked, she would kill two birds with one stone.

Taking the elevator up to the twelfth floor she located her prey's unit, and listened. From the hallway, Tuck could hear someone in the apartment. Judging by the heavy breathing, it sounded like a man. She buzzed, and a thin guy in jeans and a dirty white T-shirt answered. His hair was messy, he needed a shave, and he smelled of alcohol.

"Yeah, can I help you?" He looked at her, but didn't focus.

"I'm looking for Clarissa Morgan. Where is she?"

"Who're you?"

"I asked you a question."

"I asked you a question too, babe." He glared at her, and then looked closer. His eyes went wide with fear. She always liked the fear.

"Wait," he said. "You're a…" He didn't even bother to finish and tried to slam the door shut. Tuck blocked it easily, forcing her way in.

Nice place, she observed. *She's got good taste in everything except men.* The guy turned and ran to the back of the apartment, stumbling along the way. Tuck easily caught up in the hallway and grabbed him by the shirt collar. As she did, she heard Hugo Strange's voice in her head.

"You will enjoy the taste of flesh."

Getting a good grip, she slammed the douchebag back against the wall.

"P-p-please," he begged. "Don't." More of that delicious fear. With her razor-sharp teeth, Tuck took a generous bite out of his shoulder. He screamed, and it was annoyingly loud to her ears—all of them. So she clamped a hand over his mouth.

"Mmm, yummy," she said. "Now unless you want me to take another bite, you'll stop screaming and start to talk."

SEVENTEEN

Harvey Bullock was at his desk, having his first meal of the day—roast beef on rye—when Rick Collins rushed in.

"There's been another monster attack."

Sonuvabitch, Bullock thought. *What was I thinking, accepting this job?* Aloud he asked, "Where?"

"In The Void, but details are sketchy," Collins said. "The bodies were in such bad shape we don't even know how many people are dead."

"Well that officially ruined my appetite." Bullock pushed the sandwich aside.

"There's good news though," Collins said. "In fact, *really* good news. The responding officers found ID. It looks like one of the victims may have been a suspect in the Gotham Federal robbery."

"Wait," Bullock said. "If that's true, it means the guy's own monster took him out."

"It looks that way."

"Why would it do that?"

"Hard to say—maybe the same reason humans would,"

Collins suggested. "To take the money for themselves."

"That's possible," Bullock said, "but monsters aren't usually money hungry. Maybe hungry for something else, but they don't have much use for cash. No, it's like something else is going on here, something we don't know about yet. I wonder what that could be."

"What do you think it is?"

"If I knew it, I wouldn't be wondering, would I?" Bullock replied sarcastically. "Look, I got Mayor James breathing down my neck—he wants these things taken off the street, and pronto. Get the artist's sketches of the monsters and put out an APB. I want every available cop searching for them."

"But we've already got every available officer on monster duty."

"Doesn't matter," Bullock said. "Bring in the off-duty cops—I'll sign off on overtime pay. Keep 'em all on the street until every monster in this damn city is either dead or behind bars. *Especially* the two from Gotham Federal!"

At that Bullock sat back. He was impressed with himself—that might've been the most boss-like thing he'd done since he took this *fercockta* job. He didn't know if actions could back up his words, but…

Hey, sometimes you gotta fake it to get it right.

Without knocking, Lucius Fox entered, and he looked worried.

"What is it, Loosh?" Bullock asked.

"I need to have a word with you, Captain Bullock. It's important."

"What is it?"

"Alone would be best," Fox added.

"You can trust the kid," Bullock said. "He's my partner now."

"It's a... personal matter."

"OK, Collins, take a hike," Bullock said. "Get those cops out on the street, and pronto."

"Oh, okay," Collins said. "I'm on it."

He exited, leaving Fox and Bullock alone.

"Kids today," Bullock said, "they lack interpersonal skills. They miss all the subtle innuendos and social cues. What the hell's wrong with 'em?" When Fox didn't reply, he added, "So what's going on?"

Fox moved closer, dropping his voice. "Remember the body we pulled out of the river last week?"

"The floater that'd been in there about a week? What about it?"

"Well, we finally established an ID."

"Yeah, and who's the lucky victim?"

"His name's Rick Collins."

"You kiddin' me," Bullock said. "What're the odds? Same name as my partner." As soon as he said it, though, his eyes went wide.

"No," Fox said. "He *is* your partner."

"Sweet Jesus, Mary, and Joseph," Bullock said. "I've been working with a freakin' monster? Are you sure? How do you know Forensics didn't make a mistake?"

"With something like this, they had to be one hundred percent certain," Fox insisted. "They checked dental and medical records, and it was a perfect match."

"Jeez Louise, and I thought when Jim Gordon's double

walked in here, it was a one-time thing. We need to talk to HR about putting a better screening policy in place." Despite his joking attitude he suppressed a shudder.

"In the meantime, we have an Arkham escapee among us, at this very moment," Fox responded. "What do you propose we do about it?"

"Lemme handle it."

Bullock pulled his gun out of the desk, made sure it was fully loaded, stood and exited his office. He and Fox went down the stairs and into the vaulting room lined with metal desks. High cathedral windows let in the sunlight and sent shadows at odd angles. The Collins doppelganger was standing near his workstation, drinking coffee.

Amazing, Bullock thought. *The guy looks completely human.*

"Hey, Harv," Collins said, "I just put out that APB."

"You and me need to have a little talk," Bullock said.

"What about?"

The hell with pussyfooting. Bullock lifted his gun. "The jig's up, I know what you are. Turn around and face the desk."

Other cops were watching now. Some donned a look of shock. A murmur spread through the room.

"I... I don't know what you're talking about," Collins said. "Is this a joke?"

"Do I look like I'm joking?"

"You... you're making a mistake."

"And here I thought I was taking you under my wing," Bullock said. "Keeping you out of risky situations. Meanwhile, I was the one taking the big risk, with a monster partner." He gestured with the gun. "Let's see those hands."

"I'm not a monster," Collins protested. "You're making a big mistake?"

The guy seemed so sincere, for a split second Bullock doubted himself. His gun wavered, and Collins—or whatever the hell he was—jumped on the opportunity. In that instant he pulled his gun out, grabbed Fox, and jabbed the barrel into his cheek.

"Kill me, and I kill him." Suddenly "Collins's" eyes turned bright yellow.

Nope, no mistake.

Bullock had never understood why perps thought a standoff situation got them any leverage. He fired a single shot, right between his target's eyes. Collins's face morphed into a weird shape, melted, and then he collapsed.

"That bullet came so close to my face I felt the wind go by," Fox said, looking both shaken and indignant.

"What can I say?" Bullock smiled. "Guess we both like to live dangerously."

On the floor the body melted into a blob of yellowish green.

"There goes another partner down the well," Bullock said. Then he looked around the room. "Okay, show's over, everybody. Let's clean this mess up and get back to work."

* * *

"Jim, we gotta talk immediately."

Bullock needed a lead on the bank robbery monsters, and he knew exactly where to get it. They arranged to meet at Old City, one of Bullock's favorite watering holes. While they had spoken on the phone a bunch of times, they hadn't actually seen each other since the night the monsters had escaped from Arkham Asylum, and Gordon had driven off in Bullock's car to try to reconcile with Lee.

EIGHTEEN

Clarissa was about to open the front door to her apartment with a key when she discovered that it was already open.

Uh-oh.

"Eddie?"

No answer. The lights were on and there were empty Chinese food containers on the coffee table, along with several empty beer bottles, so she knew he was home, or had been home recently. It was possible he'd passed out in the bedroom—that wouldn't be unusual.

She was angry with Eddie for the bikers, but that didn't stop her from worrying about him. Besides, even when he messed up or did something to hurt her, she always hoped the problems would just go away. She hoped things would return to the way they had been, when they'd first met, when she felt like she was in a fairytale.

"Eddie? Are you home? Eddie?"

Everything used to be so romantic and perfect.

He'd been kind to her, and he seemed responsible and secure. He bought her flowers all the time, took her to the nicest restaurants, and loved to talk about their future. They would have kids and live in a big house in the suburbs. They would travel around the world and grow old together. When they retired they would hike together in the Himalayas.

"Eddie?"

He wasn't in the living room, but his shoes and socks were near the couch. That made it even more likely he had passed out in the bedroom. He'd been drinking a lot lately. One of his many problems.

"Eddie?" she said, a little louder this time. "Are you home?" She walked down the hallway, then stopped when she noticed dark-red spots—blood—on the floor.

"Eddie!"

She darted into the bedroom and saw him there—what was left of him—crumpled on the floor. She'd thought that seeing the two bank robbers torn to shreds had been the most horrific thing she'd ever seen, but this was worse—much, much worse.

Eddie's dying.

"Eddie!" she wailed. "I have to call you an ambulance…"

"No," Eddie said. "It's too late."

He was right. His wounds were so bad, and he had lost so much blood, she didn't see any way he could possibly survive. It was amazing that he was even alive now.

"Who did this to you?" Clarissa asked, crouching

next to him. "Was it the people you owe money to? Was it those bikers?"

"N-n-n-n-no."

"Then who?"

He tried to speak, but nothing came out. He let his head fall back, and attempted to breathe. She knew she had to call someone, call 9-1-1, get him help, but the fear was too much. She was frozen in place.

Then he lifted his head again, grimacing in pain.

"W-w-w-w-woman."

"Woman? What woman?"

"M-m-monster woman." His voice was raspy, and his breath was coming in short gasps.

Monster woman? Her mind raced. It made no sense. Both of the monsters had been men. There was no monster woman involved in the robbery. Unless she was with the loan sharks...

"G-g-g-g-g-gord—" Eddie said weakly. "W-w-wants G-Gordon."

"Gordon?" Clarissa said. "Why does she want Jim Gordon?"

Eddie said something unintelligible.

"Oh, Eddie." Clarissa started crying. "No! Please don't die. I love you so much."

"I'm s-sorry," Eddie said. "Bikers."

"Don't worry about that," Clarissa said. "Just hang on. I just want you to live. I want our future together, everything we planned for." She finally managed to stand and reached for the phone.

"I... I'm sorry. B-b-bad person. D-d-deserve bet—"

His eyes suddenly opened wider, then half closed as his head fell back, and he went still. He was dead.

"Eddie!" Clarissa wailed. "Eddie!" As she cried her emotions went wild. It was over. He was gone. There would be no more fights, no more love. No more anything. Eddie was a problem she was never going to solve.

Then a shudder rippled through her. It struck her that she had to get out of there, and fast. The monster had come for her, and it had found Eddie. Killed him. Yet where had she gone? She could still be here, hiding, waiting.

Waiting for me!

Clarissa dashed out of the room and along the hallway toward the front of the apartment. She had just entered the living room when an arm grabbed her from behind.

Ahead of her there was a mirror. In it she could see her assailant—a blond woman. She had blood all over her face and running down the front of her blouse.

She had four ears.

"Gotcha," the monster said gleefully.

"Jim!" His face brightened when he saw his old friend and partner approaching. Gordon was happy to see Bullock, too. They hugged, slapping each other's backs.

"It's great to see you, Jim."

"You too, Captain Bullock."

"Hey, even if I become president of the world someday, you can still call me Harv." Heading toward a booth, where they could have a semblance of privacy, Bullock said, "C'mon, first round's on me. I need a strong one after what I just saw." As soon as they sat down he told Gordon what had happened at Headquarters.

"I tell ya, Jim, *anybody* can be a monster," he said, shaking his head. "For all you know, I'm one right now."

"How do you know *I'm* not one, Harv?" Gordon asked.

"We've already been through that," Bullock replied. "One time's enough." A waiter came over, and they ordered their drinks—a double whiskey for Bullock, a beer for Gordon.

"To partnership, Jim." He raised his glass. "But not the kind where you gotta walk down an aisle."

"Amen to that," Gordon said, and they drank.

"You know how I know we're best friends?" Bullock said, his empty glass hitting the table. "It's 'cause no matter how much time goes by we pick up where we left off."

"I'm not sure that's the best thing," Gordon replied. "When we left off my life was in pieces, and it's not much better now."

"What're you talking about? You're making good money, ain'tcha?"

"I'm living alone in a tiny apartment. I'm alone most of the time."

"It's just a funk," Bullock insisted. "You'll get out of it soon. Besides, I offered you the chance to crash on my couch, but you didn't want to."

"I already stole your car. I didn't want to steal your apartment too."

"Ahhh, you're always welcome."

"You're the big man now," Gordon said. "You can't be seen associating with disgraced ex-cons like me."

"You're the best partner I've ever had," Bullock said, dead serious. "Which is saying a lot, and not saying a lot at the same time."

"Sounds like a toast to me."

They drank.

"Thanks, Harvey—I needed this," Gordon said. "It's been a long day, on top of a long week, on top of a long month, and it's not over. Any word on Tuck?"

"No, we're looking for her, but she's gone underground. Also looking for the monsters involved in the bank robbery." He shot his friend a look. "You don't happen to know where they are, do you?"

"How would I know that?"

"Well, you seem to have the best monster radar in Gotham."

"As usual, if I catch any monsters I'll let you know."

"That's not good enough, not anymore," Bullock said. "We've got to stop letting any of these things get away. When you're on your own, there's too much chance of that. If you have a location, you can't go in alone. You need backup."

"Yeah, but if you bring them in, I don't get the bounty."

"We can work out the details," Bullock said. "You won't get stiffed."

"Even so, I'm not working for the department anymore," Gordon said. "Don't get me wrong—I'll always do what I can to help, but I need a paycheck too. So until I'm absolutely sure, and ready to move, I have to keep my leads to myself."

"So that means you *do* have some info."

"It doesn't mean anything."

On the TV above the bar, the face of WEBG-TV news reporter Lacey White appeared. A caption announced BREAKING NEWS.

"Well look who it is," Bullock said. "My old flame." He and Lacey used to have an on-again-off-again thing going on, but the last time he had tried to see her, she blew him off. Didn't even have the courtesy to respond to his request for a booty call. Seriously, talk about the cold-fish treatment. It would've been easy to chalk it up to her loss, if she didn't look so damned good. She had long wavy dark hair and a voluptuous hourglass figure, like a star from old Hollywood.

She stood in front of an apartment building, holding a mike.

"This is Lacey White reporting live from Downtown Gotham at the scene of the latest monster-related murder."

"The hell?" Bullock said. "How does she know about this before me? Something in our system is broken, big time."

Gordon wasn't listening. He was staring at the TV.

"Just a moment ago, a man was found brutally murdered in a way that could only mean the involvement of an Arkham escapee. As yet, police haven't even arrived on the scene. We'll be covering this story live as it develops. Right now all we know is that the man was—" White stopped as if distracted by something. "Wait, my producer has just found a possible witness. Sir, sir… Can you tell us what you saw?"

A nervous-looking young guy in a hooded sweatshirt joined her in front of the camera.

"What's your name, sir?"

"Um… I, um… Do I have to give my name?"

"No, that's all right," she said, "but can you describe what you saw?"

"Yeah, I saw a monster. She was covered in blood. It was so messed up. It looked like she had a hostage or something."

Oh, crap, Gordon thought.

"Can you describe this woman?"

"She was in a dress and, um, she had double ears, like four ears total…" His eyes went wide, and he looked straight into the camera. "Wait. Is this *live*?"

"Yes." White smiled like a game show host. "We're as live as can be."

The guy darted away, off screen. White watched him go, her microphone still poised in front of her.

"It seems our witness is too apprehensive to speak, and understandably so," she said, "as all of Gotham has been lately."

"Yep, that sounds like Lacey," Bullock said. "Don'tcha th—"

Gordon stood up. "Gotta go, Harv."

"Hold on." Bullock knew exactly what had triggered his reaction. "You know where Lacey is, don't you?"

"Honestly I don't, Harv."

"What about the other monsters?"

"I told you, I don't know anything."

"If you have information you're holding back on me, Jim, that wouldn't be good. I love you, man, like a brother, but I got the safety of the public to think about, not to mention my career on the line here, so don't put me in an uncomfortable situation. I might have to—"

"Are you threatening me?"

"I'm trying not to."

Gordon put a twenty-dollar bill on the table and walked out.

"Jesus H," Bullock said. He'd lost Gordon as a partner. He didn't want to lose a friend too.

Looking at the TV screen, at "Lacey White," so pretty and perfect, it reminded Harvey of another big loss.

"Somebody, turn this goddamn thing off!"

INTERLUDE

Bruce was moving along a dark alley in Gotham. He was walking with Alfred and Selina to either side of him. Alfred was wearing a tuxedo, and Selina was in an elegant dress, heels, and a pearl necklace. They were discussing the play they had just seen.

"So what do you think?" Selina asked. "Did you enjoy it?"

"I thought it was okay," Bruce said.

"I couldn't wait for it to end," Alfred said.

"Oh, come on, Alfred, it wasn't *that* bad," Selina countered.

A man approached. He was wearing a ski mask.

"Hey, Bruce Wayne," he said.

There's something wrong here...

The voice sounded familiar. It was the voice of a teenage boy. A creepy voice that sent shivers of fear up his spine.

"What do you want?" Bruce asked.

The masked kid laughed. It was an insane laugh

and it, too, sounded familiar. Then it hit him.

Jerome Valeska.

The crazy kid from the circus who'd tried to murder him. Before Bruce could react, Jerome raised a gun...

Bruce was jolted awake, screaming. His heart was racing as if he'd been full-out sprinting. He couldn't catch his breath. It was several seconds before he could orient himself and realized that he wasn't *there*.

He wasn't in that alley.

He was in Switzerland, in the chalet.

Alfred rushed into the room. He wore an apron around his waist.

"What is it, Master Bruce?"

"It was just a dream, Alfred," Bruce said. "It seemed so real though. It was the night my parents died—yet they weren't there. You and Selina were there, and the masked killer appeared. He had a gun. It was Jerome Valeska." He shook his head to clear it.

"It seemed so real."

"Bloody hell," Alfred said, "you scared the bejesus out of me." He sat on the edge of the bed and put a hand on Bruce's shoulder. "There's nothing to worry about. Like you said, it was just a dream. The product of your imagination—maybe because we're here in the chalet. But Jerome Valeska is as dead as Churchill, and he's not coming back, mate."

"I'm not so certain, Alfred—it's not so inconceivable as we once might have thought," Bruce said. "Hugo

Strange is bringing people back to life. We've seen the proof. It makes sense that he'd want to regenerate a psychopath like Jerome. Who would make a better monster than someone who started out as one? You never know."

"What I do know," Alfred said, "is that the best thing about nightmares is that they fade in the morning light. Come to the kitchen when you're dressed. I'll have breakfast ready." He stood again and left.

Bruce got dressed and went downstairs. The house smelled of bacon and French toast. Moving into the kitchen he sat at the table, where juice and tea already sat waiting. Alfred brought over two plates laden with food, and they dug in.

"Any word about the shooter?" Bruce asked after a time.

"I was on the phone earlier, with the head of security at the resort," Alfred said. "They think the man escaped by leaving the trail and skiing down another part of the mountain. Unfortunately, there are no security cameras on the slope, which may be the reason he chose that location for the attack.

"However," he continued, after taking a drink of his tea, "the case isn't completely hopeless. The investigators have a good description of the man, and thanks to your sharp eyes they identified him from the cameras in the lift area. The police hope to have some suspects in line soon. Hopefully they'll make a quick arrest and that'll be the end of it."

"Why do you think he chose yesterday?" Bruce asked. "We've gone skiing other days."

"Killers can afford to be patient," Alfred said, "regardless of their motives. It's called playing the long game."

"Did you tell them that he spoke with a British accent?"

"Yes, Master Bruce. Unfortunately, that doesn't establish much. A great many British tourists come here on holiday, and even if he isn't a British national, he might have spent time in the UK. His accent doesn't really narrow the possibilities."

"What about his intent?" Bruce pressed. "I don't think he was out to hurt me. He shot at you first, and then threatened me. I think I was just meant to be, what do you call it, collateral damage."

"Listen to you." Alfred was smirking. "Thinking like a real detective."

"Do you have any enemies in your past?" Bruce asked.

"Enemies? That's a long list, mate." He stood suddenly. "How about some more bacon? I can make more French toast if you like."

Bruce frowned.

"I have a strange suspicion you're hiding something from me, Alfred."

Alfred turned toward the stove. With his back to Bruce, he replied, "I just don't think it's a very good idea for you to get involved, Master Bruce. This is something I should address. You have a chemistry exam to study for, and my aim remains to keep you out of trouble here in Switzerland. Well, out of any *more* trouble, that is. The last thing you need is another murder mystery, and the urge to solve it."

"Whether I was collateral damage or not, that man tried to kill me too," Bruce said. "I have a right to know what's going on."

Alfred sighed loudly, then faced Bruce again. "You make a good point, Bruce," he admitted. "All right, I guess I can allow it as this is your business now, as well as mine." He rejoined Bruce at the table.

"Before we left Gotham I received a letter in the post," he said. "It was handwritten and it had no return address, but the stamp indicated the letter had been sent from London."

"What did the letter say?"

"Well, it wasn't actually a letter, per se," Alfred said. "It was really a message, or rather a warning. It consisted of just two words. 'Remember Brussels.'"

"What happened in Brussels?"

"Actually, it began in Paris," Alfred said. "I was stationed in France for a while in my youth, and had some adventurous times. That makes it more difficult to narrow this down, but I learned long ago that the first theory that pops into your mind is usually the correct one.

"I was once involved in, let's say, an incident," he continued. "A lovers' quarrel if you will. I was in love with a woman called Gabrielle—the kind of love you can only experience in your youth. She was a smart woman, an espionage agent for the French government. We found ourselves in London, and were dining one evening at a modest Thai restaurant in Finsbury Park, when two armed men entered. It was more than a simple robbery, and as they opened fire I shot and killed them both.

"But a bullet from one of the guns struck Gabrielle in the head, killing her on the spot. I was devastated—in an instant I'd lost the love of my life. But I suppose you understand how that feels now, don't you?"

"I'm sorry, Alfred."

"You should only apologize for what you're responsible for," Alfred said. "That said, I felt responsible for Gabrielle's murder."

"Why? Maybe the men were trying to kill her. She was a spy, right?"

"No, it was all on account of me, I'm afraid," Alfred said. "The killers were hit men, hired by the brother of a Russian operative I had killed on assignment several years earlier. Feeling as I did, I had to avenge Gabrielle's death, so I hunted down and killed the man responsible—Serge Gombrovich, a Russian gangster who was living in Brussels.

"Soon thereafter I began working for your father, but I've always known that the cycle of violence and revenge wouldn't end. It rarely does in my line of work. Well, in my old line of work. Unfortunately, I was correct."

"So you think the man who shot at us is an associate of the man you killed?" Bruce asked.

"Or a member of his family," Alfred said. "More than likely this incident was personal, just as it was for me, back in Brussels. I don't expect it was a hit man, but I suppose that's a possibility as well."

"I'm guessing you didn't tell the police any of this."

"No, I told them," Alfred said. "But the Brussels incident was a very long time ago, and finding a connection won't be an easy matter. If Serge Gombrovich's family is as large and well-connected as I suspect, it will be like looking for the proverbial needle in a haystack."

"Assuming this is all connected," Bruce said, "why would he try to kill you on the ski slopes?"

"He was probably waiting for the right opportunity to get us alone. With no cameras or witnesses up there, it was the perfect spot to get away with murder. Or a double murder, had he also decided to kill you as well. All that aside, we have to be prepared. Your father installed an excellent state-of-the-art security system here, but you can never be too safe." Alfred stood and pulled up his shirt a bit to a reveal a holster and gun.

"Maybe Gotham is safer after all," Bruce said.

"I'd take my chances with a homicidal human over a homicidal monster any day," Alfred insisted. "Besides, you were the one who said you don't run away from danger, so returning to Gotham now would be running away, wouldn't it?"

"I hate it when you use my words against me."

"Ah, but they're such wise words, Master Bruce. More orange juice?"

"Yes, please."

Alfred poured the juice, then said, "We'll go back to Gotham next month, as scheduled, when you complete all your exams. I've done my part and told you the truth. For the moment, you just focus on your schoolwork. Leave the security issues to me."

Later, Alfred drove Bruce to his instructor's house on the other side of the village. More snow had fallen overnight so that everything was white and pristine, making the bright sunshine seem even brighter. They both wore dark sunglasses.

"You think you're prepared?" Alfred asked.

"I think so," Bruce said. "I was up late last night, studying the periodic table."

"I don't know how you do it, young man. When I was your age, I didn't know the periodic table from the dining room table. The thing still makes no sense to me."

"It's a tabular configuration of chemical elements, arranged by atomic number, as well as electron configuration and chemical properties."

"As I said, makes no sense, but I trust you'll do well."

Bruce's instructor, Mr. Keel, lived in a quaint two-story house on a hill and at the end of a cul de sac. The road approaching the house hadn't been plowed, so Alfred had to let Bruce out at the bottom of the hill.

"I'll be round to get you in two hours," he said. "I'll never make it up the drive, so meet me down here again. Good luck weighting those electronic elements and such."

Wearing high boots, Bruce stomped up the hill, leaving a deep furrow in the snow. It was at thigh level in some spots, so his progress was slow. Up ahead, he noticed another trail in the path, also heading in the direction of the house. Perhaps Mr. Keel had gone out that morning and left the trail himself. Stepping in those prints made the walking easier.

As he reached the house, Bruce wondered why the footprints only headed in one direction, but shrugged it off. He rang the bell and waited. After about twenty seconds, he rang again. Still no response, so he reached for the knob and turned it. The door wasn't locked, and he pushed it open.

Bruce frowned.

"Mr. Keel?"

He stepped over the threshold…

…and spotted Mr. Keel, bound and gagged in a chair, his eyes wide with fear as if silently shouting at Bruce.

"Mr. Keel!" Instinctively he moved toward his teacher.

Something sharp bit into his neck.

A moment later, his knees buckled, and everything went black.

NINETEEN

The flophouse was an abandoned building where Selina had been crashing, located in one of the seedier sections of Gotham City. When she arrived there, late in the afternoon, a bunch of kids were hanging out in front, some drinking beer and smoking. A few of them were clustered off to one side.

"Hey, Selina," a girl named Nan called out. "Where you been hiding?"

"Maybe at Wayne Manor," a guy whose name she didn't know said, giving her a wise-ass grin. They all laughed.

Selina didn't care. Unlike her, they were all a bunch of losers who were going nowhere in life. She had plans, and before long she'd be able to leave this place behind. None of them would be going with her.

She climbed the stone stairs and moved to enter the building when Nan spoke up again.

"Heard a monster almost killed you today."

Selina stopped and turned to face the girl.

"Who told you that?"

"I did."

Johnny stepped out from the group gathered off to the side. Selina hadn't noticed him before. Almost as quickly as she saw him, she turned her back on him.

"He's lying," Selina said.

"Oh, am I?" Johnny said, like he thought he was flirting.

"Actually, this guy was stalking me," Selina said, "'cause he can't handle rejection. Then a monster jumped us, and I saved *his* life."

The kids laughed. She looked out of the corner of her eye and saw that Johnny had gone bright red.

"Who shot the monster?" he said hotly.

"You did, but only after you started crying like a baby."

"*She's* lying," he insisted, his voice rising.

"I never lie," Selina said. She knew better, of course, but she really didn't give a damn. Especially when someone deserved it—and a smart-ass like Johnny definitely deserved it. So she continued up the stairs and into the building. Johnny hurried to catch up, and fell into step alongside her.

"I called in the bounty from killing that other monster," he said. "You can split the money with me if you want." Selina doubted that was the way it really happened, but she played along anyhow.

"I make my own money, thanks."

"Hey, but I was thinking—" Johnny said.

"I thought I heard a squeaking sound," Selina said, smirking.

"No, really, I'm serious," Johnny said, ignoring the dig. "I think you and me, we make a good team."

Is he flirting with me again? Selina stopped and shot him a look she *hoped* could wither plants.

"Not like that," Johnny said, holding up his hands and spreading the fingers wide. "I mean like a monster-hunting team. I think you and me, we should, like, hunt monsters together. We could make a fortune."

"No thanks," Selina said.

"Just hear me out," he persisted. "We could go after that one I just heard about on the news. Not one of the real bad-asses with wings or tentacles. This one sounds like easy money. There'd be lots of people around too, and when we kill it, there'd be plenty of witnesses. We'd get the bounty for sure."

"What the hell are you talking about?" Selina demanded. "What monster?"

"The one that just killed some guy downtown. She literally ate him alive?"

"She?" Selina said. That was a new one. At least it wasn't Dog Face. "See, you should stay away from us girls. We're dangerous."

"Tell me about it. The cops are warning everybody to stay inside till she's caught. Oh, and get this—she thinks her name's Tuck, you know like Nip and Tuck. And she has four ears. Talk about a freak show."

Wait, Tuck. That was what Fish had said, when that monster went walking into Falsettos, covered in blood. *The freak must be working with Fish.* If Tuck got arrested, Fish might go down with her.

"I'm done with monsters," Selina said to Johnny. "You're on your own, man—in more ways than one." He gaped and she turned on her heel, leaving him standing there. Walking back to the wooden stairs inside the flophouse, she went up to her space. Her mood had turned foul.

It was just a mattress on the floor and some clothes in a discarded suitcase—just a place to crash, but all Selina needed. Bruce could keep his fancy life in Wayne Manor. Selina didn't need possessions to be happy, and she didn't need people either. She liked hanging out with Bruce, Ivy, and sometimes Barbara, but if she never talked to another human being for the rest of her life she would've been happy.

One of the feral cats—an orange tiger—saw her and came running over, followed by another one. This one was solid black, without a speck of white anywhere on her body. She was Selina's favorite.

Selina could live without people, but she couldn't live without cats. They had always gravitated to her, for as long as she could remember, even since she was a little kid at the orphanage. Cats just sensed something about her, something about her personality. Since they lived on the street like she did, maybe they thought of her as a kindred spirit.

Dogs were another matter. Selina had always hated dogs. They got all clingy and emotional—*yuck*. Cats did their own thing most of the time, and generally left her alone. That's what Selina liked.

Then there was Dog Face. He was just psycho.

There was a creak on the wooden stairs. Selina hoped it wasn't Johnny coming up to bug her again. He just didn't get it. She was a solo act. Why couldn't he figure out that Selina didn't partner with anyone? Not unless there was something she could get out of it—and even then it would be short-term.

If the person was rich or powerful, Selina was willing to talk.

Johnny was neither.

It wasn't Johnny. It was Jim Gordon.

Guess Fish hasn't figured out a way to kill him yet.

"Nice place you got here," Gordon said. Could he have sounded, like, any more sarcastic?

"Works for me," Selina said. "Why do I think this isn't a coincidence?"

"We need to talk."

"I don't talk to cops. Not even ex-cops."

"I'll put this nice and simple," Gordon said. "You were involved in the bank robbery today, but if you help me, I can help you stay out of jail."

"That old trick?" she replied. "You can do better than that."

"If you're not scared, you should be."

"I don't do scared," Selina said. "Besides, if Bullock really had anything on me, the cops would've arrested me by now, or at least tried. And you're not even a cop, so why should I pay attention to anything you say?"

"Witnesses saw you at the bank."

"So I was at the bank," she said. "That's 'cause I happened to be in the neighborhood. I happen to be in *lots* of neighborhoods. That doesn't mean I was robbing it. Besides, last time I saw them, the robbers were very dead. So they're not talking."

"Clarissa Morgan can."

Crap, Selina thought, but she kept it off of her face. Was that bitch really going to rat on her?

"How do *you* know about the robbery?" Selina asked. "How do you know Clarissa Morgan? And what were you doing in The Void? You better watch out, 'cause I might tell someone *you* were one of the bank robbers. You're an ex-con, so why wouldn't people believe it?"

"Look," Gordon said, "you can keep talking nonsense, or you can cooperate. The decision is yours. But unlike you, Clarissa Morgan is a responsible member of society. Who do you think a jury will believe in a courtroom—you or her?"

Okay, Gordon really was starting to worry her.

"Responsible, yeah," she said sarcastically. "Responsible enough to rip off her own bank." He didn't say anything. "So what do you want from me anyway?" Selina asked. "I don't have any of the money if that's what you think."

"I need to know where those monsters are hiding out."

"How would I know?"

"You must have some idea." He was beginning to sound desperate.

"Maybe I do, maybe I don't," she said. "I can't decide."

"Look, I don't know who you're protecting, but I'll

tell you right now, that person doesn't give a damn about you. The monsters tried to kill you today—I was there, I saw it. So somebody out there set you up to die. Is that person worth protecting?"

Fish? Was it possible that she had set Selina up? She didn't want to believe it, but one thing Gordon had said rang true. No one gave a damn about her. She had to look out for number one.

"So if I help you, you get the bounty," she replied. "Kinda convenient, huh. So do I get a share of it?"

He thought about it, and she thought he was looking *really* nervous. There had to be something else going on.

"Agreed."

Damn, that went better than I thought.

"Okay," Selina said. "You got yourself a deal."

TWENTY

Gordon was driving and Selina sat next to him. They were headed toward The Void, to the building where Selena suspected the bank robbery monsters hung out. She was a little paranoid to be with Gordon, given that Fish might've sent that monster Tuck to kill him.

He'd done okay by her in the past, but this was a different Jim Gordon. When she first met him he was a straight shooter. There weren't a lot of cops she could trust, but somehow he always seemed like someone she could trust, at least to a point.

Now he was a bounty hunter, and while he looked mostly the same, Gordon was changed. There was an edge to him, like he was always wound up, waiting for something to happen. There was something in his eyes too—a combination of sadness and anger. Selina was good at reading people. It had helped keep her alive. Either Gordon was hard to read, or she didn't like what she saw on the page.

"You all right?" he asked.

"What do you mean?"

"You keep looking in the rearview."

"I like to make sure people aren't following me," Selina said. "It's just a habit."

"Are we going the right way?"

"Yeah, it's about a mile up ahead," she said. Then she asked, "So what happened with you and that girl, anyway? What was her name? Lee?"

Gordon seemed surprised by the question.

After a minute he replied, "It didn't go as planned."

"Too bad," Selina said. "She seemed like a cool lady."

"She still is."

"You should be careful, by the way," Selina said. "That monster that's been in the news, the one they call Tuck. I think she's after you."

"How do you know that?"

Selina wasn't going to give up Fish. She wasn't an idiot.

"I know a lot of things," Selena said. "It helps me stay alive."

They got to the house where Fish was supposed to be hanging out. It was boarded up and had signs on it identifying it as condemned. If Fish Mooney really was working with monsters, it was a safe bet there were some inside—no telling how many. And since this was close to the railroad overpass, Dog Face and his partner were likely to be among them.

Then what the hell am I doing here?

She pushed the thought to the back of her mind.

"I hope you're right about this," Gordon said. "Wait here."

No problem. Selena watched as he climbed out of the car.

Gordon took a flashlight, his gun, and the ignition key. Although Selina had agreed to help him and had been playing ball so far, he didn't exactly trust her. He hoped he was getting "good Selina" today, but with that girl, you could never be too sure. She was a good kid—well, about thirty percent of the time. The other seventy percent she liked to play both sides of a situation, and wasn't beyond double-crossing the people she supposedly liked.

Was he even on the list of the people she liked? When he'd been a cop, he definitely wasn't. Now he wasn't so sure. One thing he was certain of—Selina looked out for one person: herself. When she seemed sincere, she was probably working on some scheme to get ahead.

The closer he got to the house, the more dilapidated it looked. It looked as if no one could possibly live here, not even monsters. As he approached, a couple of rats skidded past fearlessly right in front of him. One day rats would take over this whole city, he mused. Sometimes it seemed as if they were halfway there already.

Reaching the front door, he pounded on it. The time for subtlety had passed long ago.

"Hello? Anybody in there? Hello?" He kept his gun out and was prepared to use it. After seeing the monsters tear up those two guys under the overpass, he doubted they would surrender. And there was no telling how many he'd find inside.

He banged again. "Hello?"

Three maybes crossed Gordon's mind. Maybe this wasn't the right place. Maybe Selina had screwed up. Or maybe this was a setup. He looked back and saw her sitting there in the car, watching him.

She seemed to be on the level—for now anyway.

Moving around to the side of the house, out of sight of the car, he stepped over to a dirty, partly shattered window. He peered through it into the dimly lit interior and thought he saw something moving. The way it moved wasn't human, that was for sure.

A couple of feet away there was another door. He took a few steps back, then charged it, leading with his shoulder. The old hinges snapped off easily, and Gordon was inside.

He moved quickly through the house, shining the flashlight beam ahead of him.

"Okay, we can do this the easy way or the hard way," he said loudly. "I suggest—" In that instant Gordon heard movement behind him. He turned and in the beam saw a doglike face, all ferocious teeth and drool—lots of drool. The creature barreled toward him, but Gordon was ready. He got a shot off and watched Dog Face's head practically explode.

Well, another notch on my scorecard, Gordon thought.

As the echoes of the gunshot faded, he waved the flashlight around the place. It looked worse on the inside than on the outside. Garbage, broken glass, old mattresses, and other junk were strewn everywhere, and the stench was disgusting.

He doubted Mooney spent much time here.

"These monsters have some serious hygiene issues," he muttered to himself. Continuing through the first level of the place, he said loudly, "Come on, I know you're in here somewhere. I don't particularly want to kill you, but I will if I have to. Your choice."

Off to the left he spotted something that looked newer than the piles of garbage—a large canvas bag. Moving closer, he opened it and shined the light on bound stacks of money, most likely the take from the bank robbery.

At that moment Gordon heard the front door slam. Dropping the bag he launched himself toward the sound, but tripped over something and fell. Scrambling to his feet he hurried to a window. There was the other monster, the tall one, sprinting toward Selina in the parked car.

Damn!

Waiting in the car, Selina was starting to get bored. Was this what being a cop was like? Why would anyone want to spend their lives doing this?

It was so much more exciting on the other side of the law. She could make whatever hours she wanted and, best of all, she could be her own boss, as long as she knew what she was doing.

BANG!

That was a gunshot. She didn't know what was happening inside that dump, and she just hoped Gordon got out of there alive. He'd taken the car keys with him.

CRASH!

She jumped as the front door slammed open so hard that the whole thing went flying. Then the big monster from the bank came charging out, stumbling down the stairs from the porch, stopping and glancing around frantically. It paused in front of the car and glared at Selina through the windshield like it wanted to attack her.

Seriously?

Just when she thought she was toast the monster took off, racing down the block and cutting to the left down another street.

Almost immediately Gordon came running out of the house, gun drawn, taking the stairs in one jump. He scanned the street in all directions, then came over to the car. She rolled down the passenger-side window.

"Which way did he go?"

Selina pointed. "Down there somewhere."

"*Damn!*" he said, and he seemed a lot more upset than she would have expected. Hell, he was one-for-two. What more did he expect? "Well, I got one of them," he added. "The money from the robbery's still there too. Now if only—"

"Great, I'll get it." She started to open the car

door. Gordon reached in through the window and grabbed her.

"Nice try," he said. "I already called this in, so Bullock's officers will be here before you can find where it's stashed. The money will go back to the bank, where it belongs."

He went around the front of the car and opened the door. As soon as he got in, his cell phone rang. He held it up to his ear.

"Who is this?" he demanded. Then, "How did you get my number?" He shut up and listened. "All right, I'll be right there." He ended the call and turned to Selina. His face had gone white.

"I have to go."

"Great, I'll stay here," Selina said.

"No, that's not going to happen," Gordon said. "I'll drop you closer to your place." He turned the key and revved the engine. Long before they reached the highway, he was going ninety miles per hour.

"So I only get half of one bounty?" Selina asked. "What if you get Tuck too? Do I get half of that?"

Gordon didn't answer. He just looked straight ahead, and his jaw was tight.

"I can't believe you left the bank robbery money there," Selina said. "You're not even a cop anymore. What's in it for you, staying straight? That's boring, and it's sure as hell not going to get you anywhere."

Still nothing.

She shrugged and pushed back into the seat.

* * *

They arrived at the flophouse in half the time it had taken them to drive to The Void. Being honest with herself, Selina had wondered if she was going to die, the way Gordon was driving. It was a real rush and a bummer when it came to an end.

"Get out," Gordon said.

"I don't even get a thank you?"

"Thank you."

Knowing there wouldn't be anything more, she got out of the car, and almost didn't have time to shut the door before he was speeding away.

INTERLUDE

Bruce woke up disoriented. Was he having another nightmare? Was he in Gotham?

A window came into focus—a mostly snow-covered window—and it sunk in that he still was in Switzerland. Then the events of the past two days replayed in his brain—the attack on the ski slope, Alfred dropping him off for the exam, discovering Mr. Keel bound and gagged, and then—

Bruce tried to shout. He couldn't make a sound. It registered that he'd been gagged and tied to a chair. His eyes shifted to his right and he saw that Mr. Keel was next to him, still restrained. He caught the man's eye, and they peered at each other helplessly.

When he tried to wriggle free, he couldn't budge. He was tied with ropes, and they were secured tightly. Someone knew what they were doing.

He could turn his head though, and his gaze shifted back and forth as he surveyed the room. There didn't seem to be anyone else here, and there was no sound from anywhere in the house. Whoever the person was who'd injected him with tranquilizer—most likely a member of the Gombrovich family—he appeared to have left.

Rather than trying to get free via brute force, Bruce attempted a technique Alfred had once demonstrated for him. He focused on his wrists, twisting them back and forth as much as he could. For the moment the ropes were so tight he could hardly achieve any motion at all. Over time though, he hoped they would loosen enough that he could free a hand.

The key was time. Bruce didn't know if he'd have enough time.

About ten minutes had passed, and the bindings seemed as tight as ever. And then Bruce heard a door open, then shut, and heavy footsteps approached him from behind. Though his head wasn't secured, he couldn't turn to see who was coming, and had to wait until the person appeared in his peripheral vision.

It was the blond man from the ski slope.

Without his hat and goggles, he looked older than he had yesterday. His face was weathered and ruddy. In his right hand he held a handgun.

"Ah, Bruce Wayne, up already," he said, with what Bruce thought was an upper-class British accent. "I thought you'd be out for another half hour. Nevertheless, it's a pleasure to make your acquaintance." He gave a nod.

Bruce glared at him.

"I'll assume it's a pleasure for you as well." His captor chuckled to himself, then added, "I've just been making myself at home here, having some tea." He looked at Mr. Keel. "You know, you should really keep some proper tea here. No good black tea in your entire cupboard? Well, I suppose that, since you're Swiss, you wouldn't know about tea, would you?"

Bruce muttered an epithet.

"Having trouble, Bruce? Or what does Pennyworth call you? 'Master Bruce.' So bloody subservient. Seriously, how does a grown man call a teenager 'master?' Doesn't he have an ounce of dignity? It's sad enough to take on a job serving someone else's needs twenty-four hours a day, but to humiliate himself in that way on top of it? I don't care how much money you paid me, Bruce, I would never be your butler, and I certainly would never call you, 'Master Bruce.' It's really quite pathetic."

Mr. Keel muttered something. Bruce sympathized with the sheer frustration he had to be feeling.

"Both of you are eager to get that tape off of your mouths, aren't you?" the man said. "To tell the truth, I didn't put it on you to shut you up. This house is far too isolated to allow anyone to hear you shout for help. I just didn't want to have to endure the fuss you would kick up. I've had a long several days. Hunting tires a man. I just wanted a little peace and quiet.

"That all said," he continued, "I'm willing to strike a deal with you. I'll remove the tape, but you have to agree to control yourselves. If you raise your voices beyond an acceptable level—just one time—the tape goes back on... permanently.

"Do we have a deal?"

Both Bruce and Mr. Keel nodded.

"Very well then."

He went over to Mr. Keel and, with a swift and vicious movement, tore off the tape. Bruce's tutor had facial hair, and without a doubt the tape took a lot of it. Bruce winced with sympathy, and in knowing what was to come.

Keel groaned in agony.

"Hey, what did I just tell you?" the man said, a hint of amusement in his voice.

"You bastard," Keel said.

"That's the thanks I get," the man said, then he turned. "Ah, don't worry, Bruce, I didn't forget about my little billionaire." He stepped over, and with a sudden jerk ripped off the tape covering Bruce's mouth. The pain was excruciating, as if someone had torn off his lips, yet he refused to give a reaction or make a sound. Gulping air, he took a few moments to compose himself.

"What do you want from us?" he asked.

"Oh, come now," the man said. "You know I don't want anything from *you*. I thought you were smarter than that. Perhaps this elite schooling you're getting is going to waste."

"All right, then," Bruce said. "What do you want from Alfred?"

"Ah, now, don't you see? *That's* more like it. There's hope for you yet, Bruce." The man shook his head. "I'm afraid, though, that my quarrel with Pennyworth is none of your concern. You're simply what's known as bait."

"Whatever you want, you won't get it."

The man laughed, and the more he did, the harsher it became. The laughter lasted for about a minute and brought tears to his eyes.

"My goodness," the man said. "I haven't laughed like this in ages." He wiped the corners of his eyes. "Thank you, Bruce. I *really* needed that."

Bruce and Keel had remained stone-faced.

"I won't get it." The man laughed again, though briefly. "That's brilliant. I won't get what I want, says the scrawny teenage boy bound to a chair."

"I could beat you in a fight," Bruce gritted. "Untie me like a man, and I'll show you."

"'Untie me like a man, and I'll show you,'" their captor mimicked. "As tempting as that sounds, I think I'll pass."

"We still don't know what you want from us," Keel said. The poor fellow was a complete innocent in this scenario, and utterly oblivious.

"It's all quite simple," the man said. He began pacing back and forth in front of the two bound captives, still holding the handgun. "When Pennyworth arrives to pick up his 'master,' we'll see if he's willing to trade his life for Bruce's." He glanced down at his watch, then back up. "In other words, we'll find out if he really considers you his 'master,' when his own life is on the line. I suspect what we discover will cause him substantial pain."

"Alfred has always been willing to risk his life for me," Bruce said. "And I'm entirely willing to do the same. That's what friends do."

"So you consider Pennyworth your friend as well as your subordinate?" their captor said. "It's a fascinating relationship you two have, really."

"What about my life?" Keel said. "Will he trade his life for mine as well?"

"Oh, right," the man said. "At this point, professor, I'm afraid you are what we call a loose end." He casually lifted the gun, aimed it at Keel and squeezed the trigger. There was a deafening *bang*, all the more startling in the quiet setting. A bullet entered Keel's forehead and exited the back, splattering blood and brains onto the wall behind him.

It killed him instantly.

"No!" Bruce shouted in horror. "Why did you do that? He didn't have anything to do with this. *Why did you kill him?*"

He didn't really expect an answer.

"It's a shame you won't have a chance to take your chemistry test today," the man said. "I'm sure you would've received an A."

"You're going to pay for this," Bruce said, tears streaming down his cheeks—as much from anger as from sorrow. "*I'll make sure you pay!*"

The man laughed, then stopped himself. "Please,

don't get me started again. If I laugh any more today, I don't think I'll be able to stand it." He tucked the gun into his belt. "Can I get you anything while we wait? I'd offer you tea?"

After a time, Bruce did need something—he needed to use the bathroom.

"I need to pee."

He didn't expect the man to release him, but decided to try it, to see if his captor was cocky enough—or stupid enough—to free his arms and legs.

"I'm sorry," the man said, "but I'm afraid you'll have to hold it in or wet your pants. Those are your only two options." Then he smiled broadly. "If you'd like a piece of chocolate, however, I'll get you some. It's actually quite good. Not as good as British chocolates, of course, but nothing is."

"I don't want your food."

"It's not my food," the man said. "It's your teacher's food. You don't want to insult him, do you? I mean, he's having a rough day."

Bruce spat at the man. It landed on the man's arm, and he nonchalantly wiped it off. His expression didn't change.

"I'll take that as a definitive no."

Time passed with excruciating slowness. Bruce remained stubbornly stoic, not uttering a word. He fought to avoid looking at his dead teacher, but the gruesomeness slumped in the chair next to him was unavoidable. In the absolute silence of the house, he could hear the occasional drip of blood that fell to pool on the floor.

Alfred had taught him that an opportunity would always present itself, enabling him to regain the upper hand. The key was to remain calm under pressure, so that when the opportunity came along, he would be ready to take advantage of it. So his mind raced from scenario to scenario, all designed to get him free and give him the upper hand.

All of them ended in disaster.

He jerked his head up when he heard a car horn. It honked several times, and Bruce knew that Alfred had arrived.

His captor knew, too.

"Sounds like your butler is here," he said, peeking through the window. "The sun is still shining, and quite brilliantly. This has turned into a beautiful day, indeed."

"If you let me use my phone, I can call Alfred and tell him to come to the house."

"Of course," the man said. "That's a lovely offer. Thank you for making it, but I'd rather you didn't have the chance to warn him of what awaits."

"If Alfred leaves you won't get your chance," Bruce said. "He'll assume I went home ahead of him and drive off."

"There's no reason for Pennyworth to think that, and he won't leave you," the man said. "Even if he does, I'll just kill you, bury you with your unfortunate teacher, and move to an alternative plan. As long as you don't appear, he'll remain within my reach. I believe it's what you Americans call a 'win-win situation.'"

"In the meantime," he added, "it's time to shut you up again." He picked up a roll of duct tape, stepped over to Bruce, and wrapped the tape over his mouth and around his head.

Bruce knew he was right. Alfred wouldn't leave, and he'd come to house. He would suspect that something was "off" about the situation. Bruce prided himself on being reliable, doing whatever he said he was going to do. When that didn't happen, Alfred's guard would be up.

The car honked several more times.

Then a long silence.

Pulling back the curtain, the captor peered out the window. "Ah, here comes the man. I wish I was a better shot—I'd kill him right now."

Bruce heard footsteps crunching in the snow. Following the tracks he'd left. The bell rang.

Gun in hand, the man went to answer the door. Trying to time it perfectly—a moment before the door opened—Bruce shifted all of his weight to one side. At precisely the right moment he and the chair tipped over, landing with a *crash*.

It worked.

As the door began to open, Alfred rammed it hard, right into the man's forehead. The man stumbled backward and fell to the floor with a cry. Pushing into the room, Alfred grappled with the man, and the gun clattered off to one side.

With furious purpose Alfred's opponent lurched upward, forcing Alfred backward and off-balance. His shoulders hit the wall and he used it to steady himself, then pushed forward again. Still groggy from the impact, the man wasn't prepared for the quick response.

He swung at Alfred, who easily dodged the attempt. Then Alfred responded with a rapid uppercut that caught the man full on the jaw. His head snapped back, his eyes rolled up, and this time when he hit the floor, he didn't get up.

Making sure his opponent was, indeed, unconscious, Alfred scanned the room. His jaw clenched when he saw Bruce, bound and gagged, then his eyes went wide when he spotted the corpse. Crossing the distance quickly, he knelt next to Bruce and removed the tape from his mouth.

"Owwwww," Bruce responded.

"Are you all right, Master Bruce?"

"A lot better than I was a minute ago."

Quickly and efficiently, Alfred untied the ropes that had been restraining Bruce's arms. Then he made short work of the ones holding his legs. As he did, he peered at the bloody mess in the adjacent chair.

"Bloody hell," Alfred said. "I presume my blond tormentor did this to you?"

"He did," Bruce said. "Do you have any idea who he is?"

"Not a fucking clue."

There was movement beyond Alfred's shoulder, and Bruce saw the blond man reach for his gun and rise into a crouch.

"Alfred, behind you!"

"You bastard," the man groaned. He lifted the gun, trying to aim it, but was still groggy. Alfred lunged toward him and grabbed his hand—the one gripping the gun. A shot rang out and the bullet went into the ceiling, sending down a dusty cloud of plaster.

Bruce struggled to free himself the rest of the way.

The men continued to struggle. His opponent had the advantage of weight, but Alfred's head was clear. He squeezed the man's wrist, forcing him to keep the gun pointed upward. Two more shots fired into the ceiling.

"Who the hell are you?" Alfred growled.

"You murdered my father," the man replied. "I am Alexi Gombrovich. I was ten years old when you killed him. I vowed to one day get my revenge." His words seemed to fuel his rage, and he pushed Alfred back. "Well, today's the day."

"Your father caused an innocent woman to be killed in a crossfire," Alfred responded. "He was responsible for many other deaths. If I didn't kill him someone else would have."

"My father was a professional."

"Rubbish. Your father was an evil man."

"You're wasting your breath, Mr. Pennyworth. None of your lies will prevent me from killing the both of you."

"Your quarrel is with me, not the boy."

"Two lives in exchange for one," Alexi replied, "and the destruction of my world. It's a fair trade." Fueled by his fury he gained the upper hand. The gun hand lowered, and slowly, inexorably, he turned the weapon toward Alfred.

Then Bruce's hands were free. He lunged from the chair and tried to tackle Alfred's opponent, but Alexi shoved him away. All three men were thrown off balance. Jerking his hand free in the tussle, he aimed the gun at Bruce.

Instinctively Bruce turned his head to the side. He saw Mr. Keel's body, his ruined face, and prepared himself for the same fate.

Sure enough, a shot was fired.

But there was no pain.

He faced the combatants again and saw Alexi, stumbling backward. A bright-red stain blossomed on his shirt, coming from a wound in his chest. He wore a look of shock, and then all awareness fled his eyes. He dropped the gun and collapsed.

Alfred let him fall and moved over to Bruce.

"You all right, mate?"

"I'm fine," Bruce said. "Thank you."

"I think I should be the one doing the thanking. Looks like the training is paying some dividends."

"It didn't help Mr. Keel," Bruce said somberly.

The local police arrived a short time later. There was a lot of questioning, facilitated by the fact that the officers spoke fluent English, and they seemed entirely satisfied with the account of the events. It fit with what Alfred had revealed to them before.

Finally, they were allowed to leave. As they drove back to the chalet, Bruce was in a somber, reflective mood.

"It never gets easier," Alfred said. "Witnessing a death—especially the death of someone for whom you care—leaves an indelible mark. It's something you'll carry with you. You just have to mourn and soldier on."

"Mr. Keel told me he had a son," Bruce said. "Just seven years old. I keep thinking about how that boy is going to feel when he finds out that his father has been killed. He'll feel the way I felt. An enormous void will open in him, and it can never be filled." He turned to face his friend. "It's all our fault, Alfred."

"That's not true."

"If it wasn't for us, that boy's father would be alive right now," Bruce persisted. "He wouldn't have to go the rest of his life, feeling that void."

"You can't take responsibility for all of the horror in the world," Alfred said. "If you do, you'll go mad. At the same time, you should be proud of yourself—you have genuine empathy. Not many people these days do."

As they continued driving along, the snow glistened in the late afternoon sun. Looking at the seemingly endless vistas, it was hard to believe that such darkness existed in the world. Everything seemed so peaceful and pristine.

* * *

Back at the chalet, Bruce and Alfred didn't speak. It was as if all the words had been said, and there was nothing more to discuss. Instead, they began packing.

It was time to return to Gotham.

TWENTY-ONE

"Harvey, I just got one of the bank robbery suspects." Gordon told Bullock where the cops could find the body, at the house in The Void. "Tall one got away. Oh, also, I'm going to need backup at Wayne headquarters, but you have to be discreet. Otherwise a hostage will be killed."

He was driving as fast as he dared, using his phone on speaker so he could keep both hands on the wheel. It was full-on night.

"I'm on my way there now."

"What's going on at the Wayne building?" Bullock asked.

"Tuck's there," Gordon replied.

"Tuck? The monster chick?" Bullock growled. "First one of the bank robbery suspects, now you got Tuck. I thought you didn't have any info?"

Gordon didn't reply at first.

"I guess I lied."

"Son of a bitch," Bullock said.

Gordon ended the call. He was almost there.

The side streets were relatively empty, so parking wasn't a problem. He sprinted up the concrete steps and entered through the revolving doors. From his time on the force, he'd gotten to know Carlos, one of the nighttime guards. He was at the front desk. Behind him monitors displayed security footage from various locations in the building.

"Hey, Jim Gordon," Carlos said. "Been awhile."

"Hey, Carlos, I need to check something out."

"I thought you weren't with the GCPD anymore?"

"I, um, do some freelance work for them," Gordon lied. "This is official business."

"Oh, okay," Carlos said. He hesitated for a second, then nodded. "You can go on up."

"Thanks." Gordon gestured toward the monitors. "Anyone else go up there recently? Maybe to the top floor?"

"No, not a soul," Carlos said, and then he swiveled around in his chair to look at the screen. "Hey, that's weird—it looks like the video feed is frozen up. I gotta call this in."

"Do that, then stay down here and watch your back," Gordon said. "There could be a monster loose in the building."

"A monster? Wait, you sure you wanna go up there alone?"

"I've got it under control," Gordon said.

Carlos reached for the phone on the desk, and Gordon headed toward the elevator banks. Choosing the appropriate one, he hit the button for the top floor. Given GCPD response time, he didn't have long to nab this monster.

Getting off at the last stop, he found the stairs to the roof. Letting the door close as quietly as he could, he took them two at a time. With his gun drawn, he gingerly pushed open the second door, and stepped outside. He scanned for any sign of movement.

There was no one there.

Then he heard, "Over here."

Spinning to his left he saw Tuck as she emerged from behind a large environmental unit. Since the majority of the building was empty, the machine was silent. Gordon cursed inwardly. That meant Tuck would have heard him coming a mile away.

He saw Clarissa, too. They stood near the ledge overlooking the street, and Tuck gripped her hostage firmly around the waist. Another hand held her arm.

"Let her go," Gordon said. He raised his gun.

"Shoot, and we'll both die," Tuck growled. "Even if you hit me, I'll drag her over the edge. I've got nothing to lose and everything to gain, you sonofabitch."

Gordon lowered his gun.

"What do you want?"

"Your death," Tuck said.

"Not going to happen," Gordon replied. "I've already called GCPD. The cops are on the way—there's no chance you can escape. Give it up while you're still alive."

"But I'm not alive," Tuck said. "Not any more. You took away the one person who made my life worth living. I want yours in return, and I want you to suffer." She tightened her grip on Clarissa's arm, and the young woman whimpered. A spot of blood appeared where a claw broke through.

"You didn't love Nip," Gordon said, "you were just programmed to love him." He didn't know if this was true or not, but he hoped that saying it would throw her off-balance, cause her to make a mistake of some sort.

"That's a lie," Tuck said. "I know how I feel, how *he* felt. It was real—as real as anything in this world. Thanks to you, it's over."

"Hugo Strange is your enemy, not me," Gordon said, "and certainly not Clarissa. Just do the right thing. Have faith that maybe, just maybe, we're playing for the same team." For a brief moment, Gordon thought he was getting through to the monster. He thought he saw a spark of—was it humanity?—in her eyes.

Then, as quickly as the spark had appeared, it vanished.

"Strange is a great man," she said. "*You're* my enemy. You and all the other people I need to kill."

"For the last time," Gordon said. "Let her go."

"Don't you get it?" Tuck said. "The game's over. You can't win." Before he could react, she bit into Clarissa's neck, her huge, sharp teeth glistening in the ambient light of the city. She must have severed the artery because blood gushed from the wound and out of Clarissa's mouth. Clarissa never uttered a sound, but her eyes showed the shock.

"*Noooo!*" Gordon bellowed.

He started forward, and Tuck let go of her victim. Even as Clarissa crumpled onto the rooftop, Tuck was in motion, lunging to meet Gordon in his charge. He fired, hitting her in the shoulder, but the bullet went clear through and she didn't hesitate.

She hit him like a freight train, grabbed him by the arms, and they fought, struggling to remain on their feet on the roof's gravelly surface. Unable to bring his firearm up for another shot, he wrestled with all of his strength. It was like being caught in twin vices, and he could hardly move.

"It'll take more than a bullet to kill me," Tuck said. "I'm already dead—you can't kill me again. There's nothing can stop me from tearing you to pieces, bit by bit, while you scream for mercy.

"Mercy is something you'll never get," she added. Tuck bit at his neck, and he narrowly twisted out of the way. Then he threw himself to one side, using his weight to unbalance her, and they hit the rooftop. He flipped her over, gaining the advantage. She lost her grip on one arm.

"You're pretty lively for a dead woman," Gordon said. "A lot more lively than Nip was when that chandelier landed on him." He hoped his words would cause her to lose control, allowing him to put some distance between them. One bullet might not have done the trick, but there were more where that one came from.

It didn't work. She wrenched the gun out of his hand and flung it away. *Damn*, she was strong. Then she grabbed him again in that vice-like grip, picked him up off his feet, and tossed him over her head, slamming him down onto the tar roof. He was lucky she was so enraged. Had she thought about it, he'd be hurtling toward the street below.

Gordon made it up onto his knees, but before he could stand she was there, looming over him. Her mouth opened, wider than he could have imagined, as she prepared to bite off his face. This wasn't the fate he had envisioned when he chose this new career, but he supposed he should have expected it.

Using his legs, he pushed Tuck backward in a last desperate effort. Her feet ground in the gravelly tarpaper used to surface the roof, and she resisted his pressure. Then she gasped and her leg flew out from under her as she slid on Clarissa's blood, which had pooled around the body. Startled into releasing her grip, Tuck pinwheeled her arms and tried to grab him again, but he twisted out of the way.

In the next instant, she plunged out of view.

Without regard for what happened to Tuck, Gordon moved quickly to where Clarissa lay. She had lost an amazing amount of blood, but somehow she was still breathing. Every breath caused her to whimper with pain though.

"Hold on," Gordon said. "Hold on…"

She tried to say something. Her mouth opened, but she couldn't speak. Then he realized that holding on was the worst thing she could do. Trying to live was causing her too much agony, and it was a battle she wasn't going to win.

"Don't give up," he said. "Keep fighting." Her lips moved again as she tried to speak.

"Help, Carlos, somebody!" he bellowed, but it was too late. Her lips quivered one last time, then went still. Her eyes went blank.

"Damn it, *no*."

He held her hand, hoping she was in a better place. Given the state of the city these days, it wouldn't take much.

TWENTY-TWO

Sitting at her table in the back of Falsettos, Fish watched the television on one wall. From outside Wayne Tower, Lacey White reported on Tuck's death.

Selina stood behind the bar.

"Gotham is a little bit safer tonight," White said with a smug grin.

Fish laughed bitterly. "Yeah, right."

White continued. "The monster who went by the name of 'Tuck' was killed this evening during a fight with former GCPD detective James Gordon. Authorities have confirmed that Gordon, himself an ex-convict, was responsible for the killing of Tuck's partner, Nip. The two were said to have been given their identities by their creator, Hugo Strange."

"James Gordon," Fish said, and she twisted her lip. "A thorn in my ass."

"He's not such a bad guy," Selina said. "I mean, I've seen worse."

"Well, I suppose the old adage is true," Fish said.

"If you want something done right, don't send a goddamn monster to do it." She had a good run with Tuck though, and there were more where she and her partner had come from. In the end, however, monsters were no better than regular people. And when your assets stopped delivering what you needed from them, you had to toss them away and move on.

Speaking of which...

"Big Guy!" Fish called out. The towering creature with the deformed back was in the lounge area, where he sat in the shadows doing his best to be unobtrusive. Hearing her call, he rose and walked over, towering above her.

"Give me your hand," Fish said.

He obeyed, and she gripped it.

"Let's see if, unlike your dimwitted partner in crime, you can complete a simple task for me," she said. A flash of pain throbbed in her head. "Go to Mishkin's Pharmacy and bring me some medicine." She wrote it down on a slip of paper. "It's an immunosuppressant. You know, the same one you got for me last time. You can complete this simple task for me, can't you?"

Big Guy grunted. She took this as a yes. He turned and stalked out of the club, leaving through a side door. Selina and Fish watched as the door closed behind him.

"They're so gross," Selina said.

"Yet useful," Fish said. "At least when they do what they're supposed to do."

"So this is what your plan is? To keep working with monsters?"

"Why not? We can't let a couple of bumps in the road stop us. Hell, I *died*, and yet I'm still here. When you hit some adversity in life, you've got to dig deeper, find the strength to continue. So, Selina Kyle, are you with me?"

Selina didn't even have to think about it.

"I'm with you."

"Then to the future." Fish raised her glass. "It's going to be stupendous." She swallowed the rest of her drink and tossed the glass somewhere behind her, letting it shatter.

EPILOGUE

Gordon's phone rang. He was lying on his couch, icing one of his many wounds, still rattled from watching Clarissa die. He was going to let the call go to voice mail, then he glanced at the display.

He grabbed for the phone and jabbed "answer."

"What's the good news, Harvey?"

"Feeling optimistic for a change, huh, Jim?"

"No, just trying to be less pessimistic."

"Well, this might help—in a way. I've got a present for you… sorta," Bullock said. "There's a lead on the monster that escaped, the one from the bank robbery. We got a call that the monster was just seen breaking in to Mishkin's Pharmacy."

"So why isn't the GCPD heading down there?"

"Figured I'd give you a shot at another bounty," Bullock said. "Least I can do for taking out Tuck and the other monster today. Especially given the circumstances."

Gordon flashed back on the sight of Clarissa's body as the life drained out of it. No matter how often he saw that kind of thing, it never became normal. He hoped it never would.

"Isn't it against the law to give me a lead?"

"Hey, just 'cause I'm a cop doesn't mean I'm some kinda law expert," Bullock said. "I'm still pissed off that you played fast and loose with the truth, Jim, but you deserve this bust. And a guy's gotta earn a living—especially without the perks that come with a badge."

Gordon's entire body ached, but he managed to pull himself up off the couch.

As he arrived at Mishkin's, a body came flying through the window, sending fragments of glass everywhere and landing on the sidewalk with a sickening thud. Then the big guy, Marino, exited the store and snarled at him.

"Hey," Gordon said, "any chance you want to come quietly?"

Marino just grunted, then launched himself at Gordon. He was at least as strong as Tuck, and just as vicious. Grabbing Gordon, he easily hurled him into the street.

Crap, this is just what I don't need right now. Scrambling to his feet, Gordon watched as his opponent stepped out into the street as well.

Right into the path of a speeding oil truck.

Not that long ago, this would've been one of the most gruesome deaths he'd ever witnessed. Now it didn't make the top ten. He moved over to where the pharmacist lay, expecting to find the worst. But the man was moving, and he groaned.

"You okay?" Gordon asked.

"Yeah." The guy looked dazed, but he'd be okay. "Thank you."

Once the cops had finished with the paperwork—something he would *never* miss—he suppressed a combination of a sigh and a groan. Now his injuries had injuries, and whenever he moved everything complained.

This one had been a win all round though. He'd saved the pharmacist's life, and he could claim a bounty as a bonus. The guy who hit the monster had just kept on going, probably figuring he'd be chased for hit-and-run. He'd be looking over his shoulder, and technically he deserved to.

Still, there was one less victim of the monster crisis.

It didn't ease the pain of failing to save Clarissa.

But it was something.

There were a lot more Arkham inmates on his list, and more than ever he intended to catch them all. Every victim just served to drive him that much more—not since he'd given up his badge had he felt such a sense of purpose. He knew that this was a rebound job for him, not a career but a distraction to help him forget about Lee and the life he'd lost.

In his heart, he knew he was still a cop. Somehow, some way, he'd get back to that. As he walked away, the pharmacist called out to him.

"Hey, who are you anyway?"

Gordon stopped and turned back.

"I'm Jim Gordon," he said. "I used to be…" He stopped, and thought about it.

"I'm a bounty hunter."

Yeah, that sounded pretty good.

For the time being, anyway.

ACKNOWLEDGMENTS

Huge thanks to my outstanding editor, Steve Saffel, and the entire *Gotham* team at Warner Bros. and the Fox television network.

ABOUT THE AUTHOR

JASON STARR is the international bestselling author of many crime novels, thrillers, graphic novels, and comics. His novels include *Cold Caller*, *Twisted City*, *The Follower*, *Panic Attack*, *The Pack*, and *Savage Lane*. He has also co-authored the four-book "Bust" series of novels with Ken Bruen for Hard Case Crime. His work in comics for Marvel and DC has featured Wolverine, The Punisher, Sand, The Avenger, Doc Savage, and Batman. In addition, for Marvel he authored the original prose novel, *Ant-Man: Natural Enemy*. In 2017, Titan Books published Starr's first official Gotham novel, *Gotham: Dawn of Darkness*.

Starr has twice won the Anthony Award for mystery fiction, as well as the Barry Award. His next thriller, *Fugitive Red*, will be published in November 2018 in the US and Europe. He lives in New York City. Connect with Starr at

www.jasonstarr.com and
twitter.com/JasonStarrBooks

For more fantastic fiction, author events,
competitions, limited editions, and more

VISIT OUR WEBSITE
titanbooks.com

LIKE US ON FACEBOOK
facebook.com/titanbooks

FOLLOW US ON TWITTER
@TitanBooks

EMAIL US
readerfeedback@titanemail.com